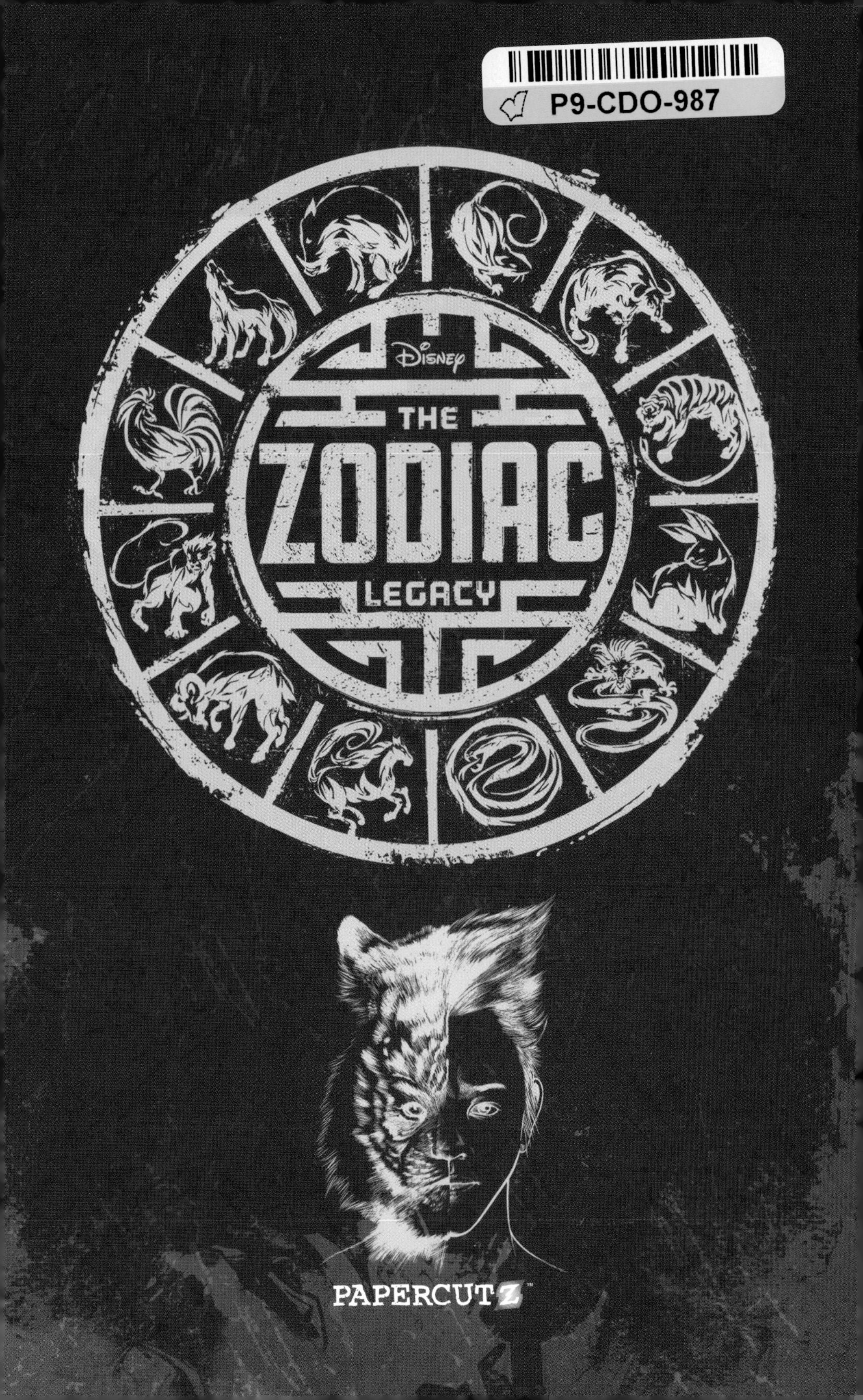
Disney
THE
ZODIAC
LEGACY
PAPERCUTZ

Disney Graphic Novels available from PAPERCUTZ

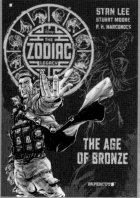

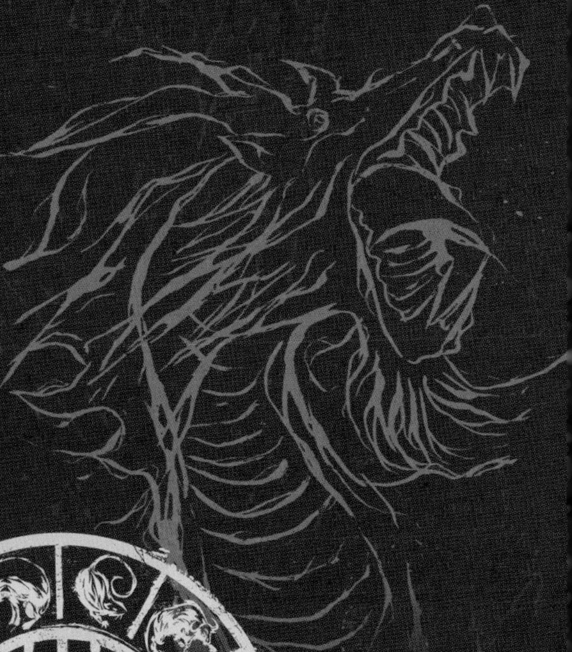

Disney

THE ZODIAC LEGACY

#3 "The Age of Bronze

Stan Lee – Creator

Stuart Moore – Writer

P.H. Marcondes – Artist

PAPERCUTZ

New York

#3 "The Age of Bronze"
Stan Lee – Creator
Stuart Moore – Writer
P.H. Marcondes – Artist
Andie Tong – Cover, Endpapers, and Character Profiles Artist
Jolyon Yates – Title Page Artist
Laurie E. Smith– Colorist
Bryan Senka – Letterer
Dawn Guzzo – Design/ Production Coordinator
Jeff Whitman – Editor
Jim Salicrup
Editor-in-Chief

ISBN: 978-162991-484-8 paperback edition
ISBN: 978-162991-485-5 hardcover edition

Papercutz books may be purchased for business or promotional use. For information on bulk purchases please contact Macmillan Corporate and Premium Sales Department at (800) 221-7945 x5442.

Printed in Korea
July 2017

Distributed by Macmillan
First Printing

The power of the Zodiac comes from twelve pools of mystical energy. Due to a sabotaged experiment, twelve magical superpowers are unleashed on Steven Lee and twelve others.

TIGER

STEVEN

POWERS:

STRENGTH, REFLEXES

Now Steven Lee is thrown into the middle of an epic global chase. He'll have to master strange powers, outrun super-powered mercenaries, and unlock the secrets of the Zodiac Legacy. When Steven is first rescued by Jasmine and Carlos, he relishes his newfound powers and is excited to be on a grand adventure, alongside...

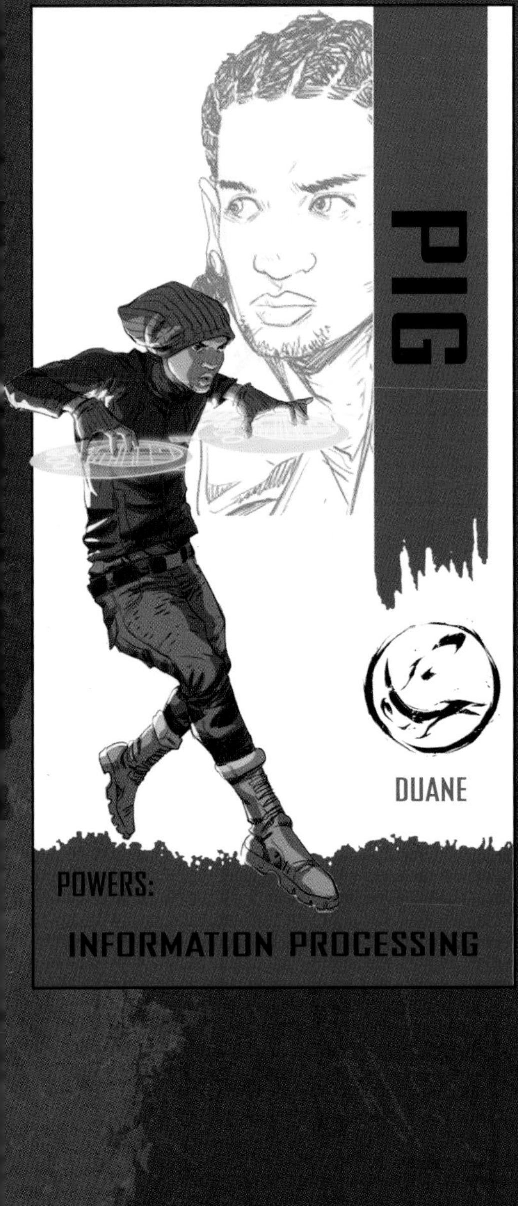
PIG
DUANE
POWERS:
INFORMATION PROCESSING

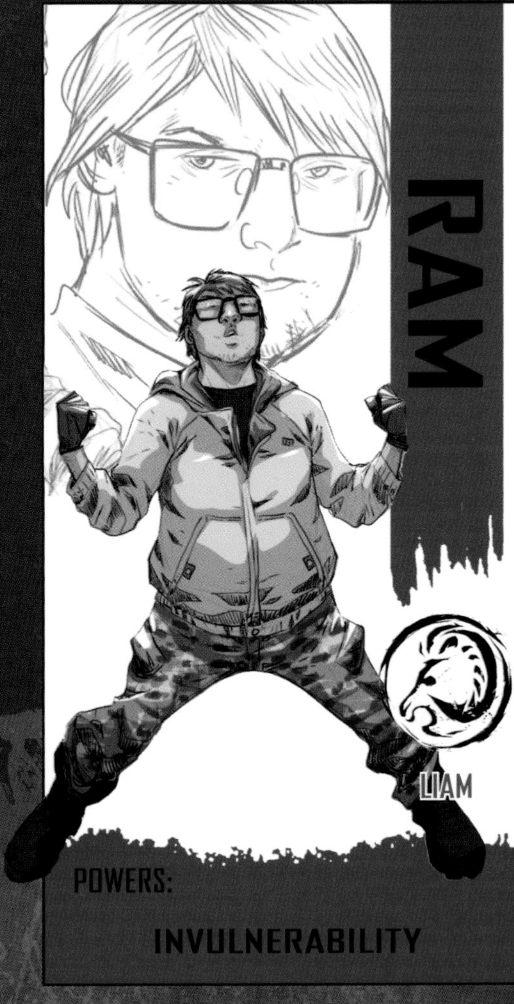
RAM
LIAM
POWERS:
INVULNERABILITY

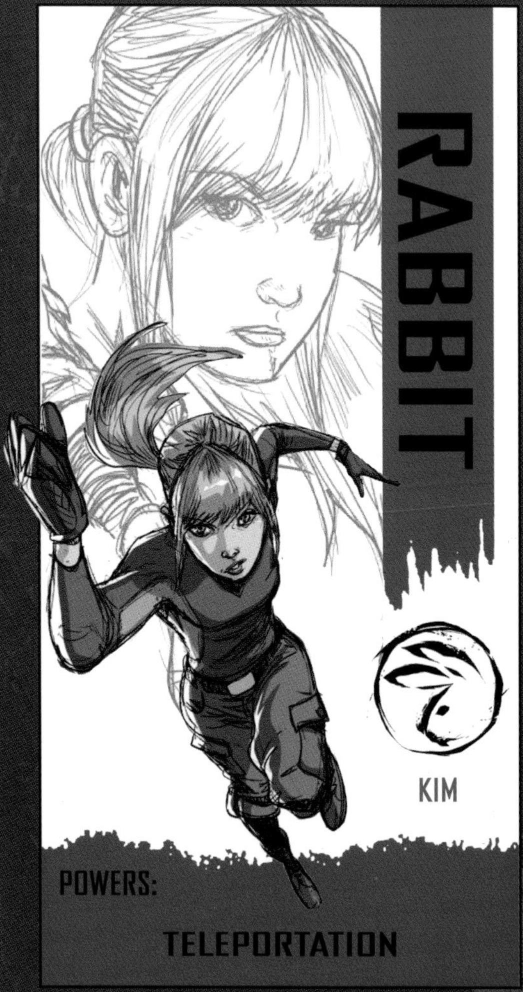
RABBIT
KIM
POWERS:
TELEPORTATION

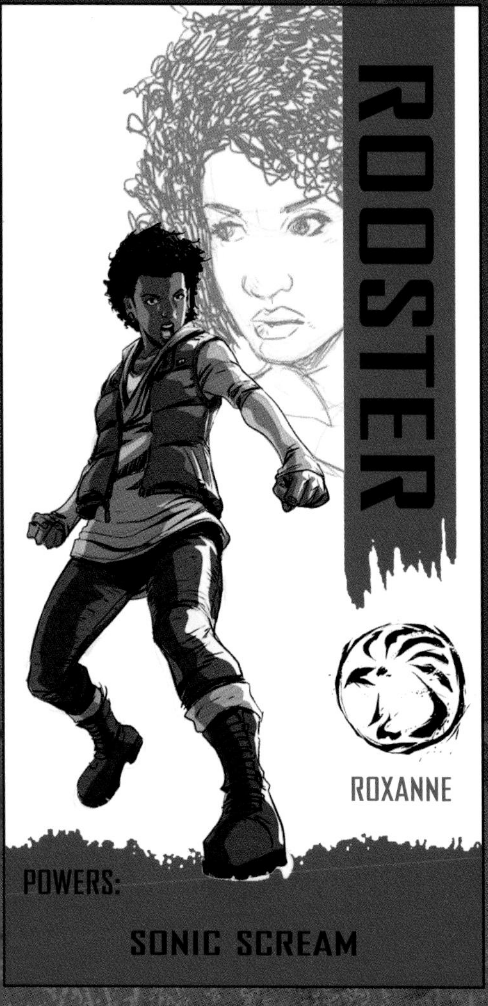
ROOSTER
ROXANNE
POWERS:
SONIC SCREAM

DRAGON

JASMINE

POWERS:
FIRE BREATHING, FLIGHT,
MIND CONTROL

Steven and his new friends
will need to stay one step
ahead of the Vanguard...

DRAGON

MAXWELL

POWERS:
FIRE BREATHING, FLIGHT,
MIND CONTROL

Maxwell and the
Vanguard organization
is bent on tracking
down all of the Zodiac
powers. The Vanguard
are...

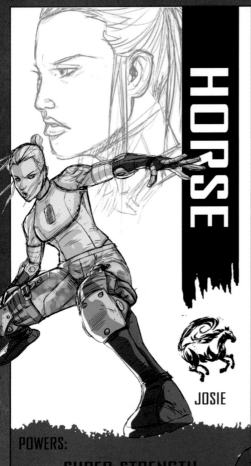

HORSE

JOSIE

POWERS:

SUPER STRENGTH
AND ENDURANCE

OX

MALIK

POWERS:

STRENGTH

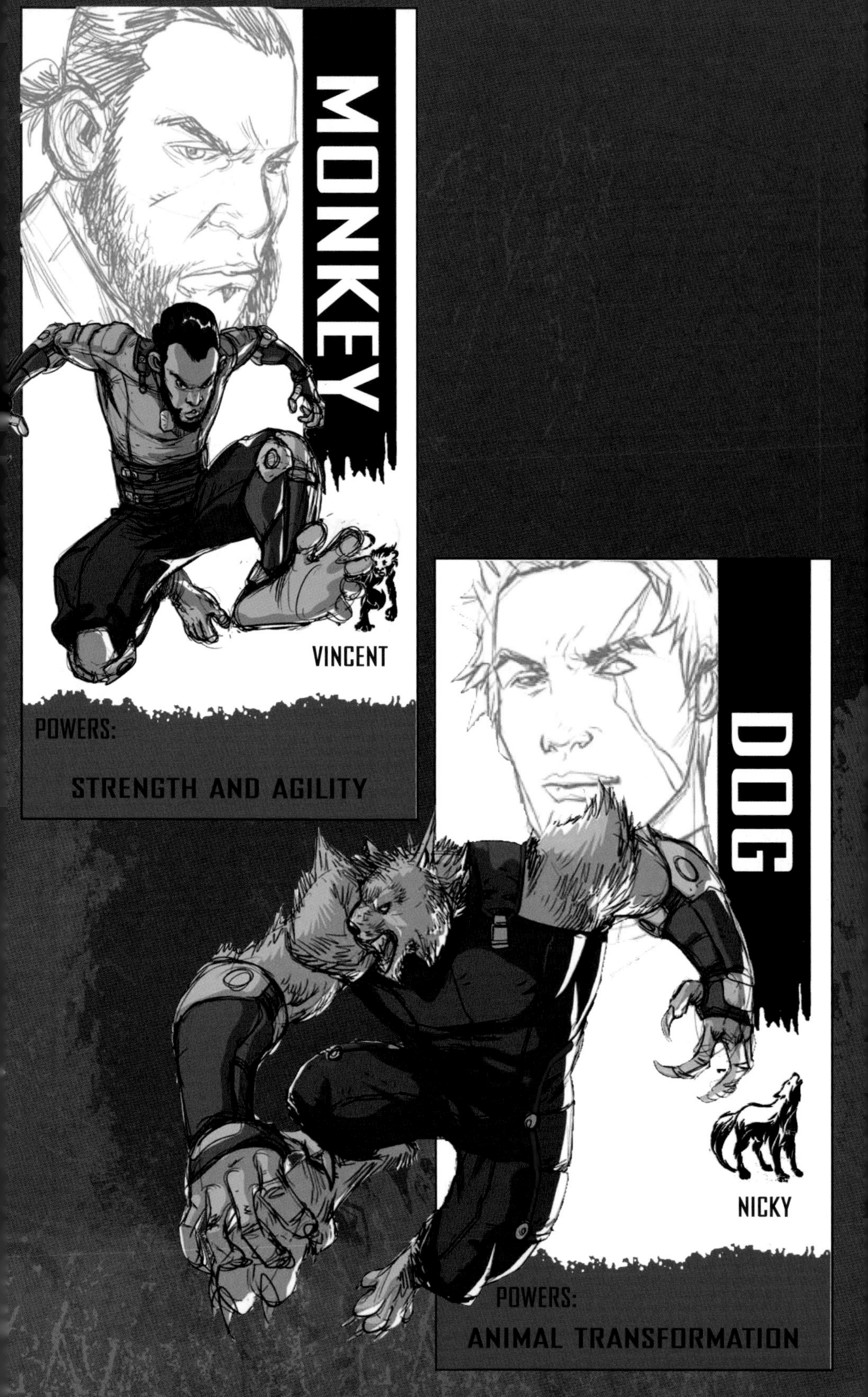
MONKEY
VINCENT
POWERS:
STRENGTH AND AGILITY
DOG
NICKY
POWERS:
ANIMAL TRANSFORMATION

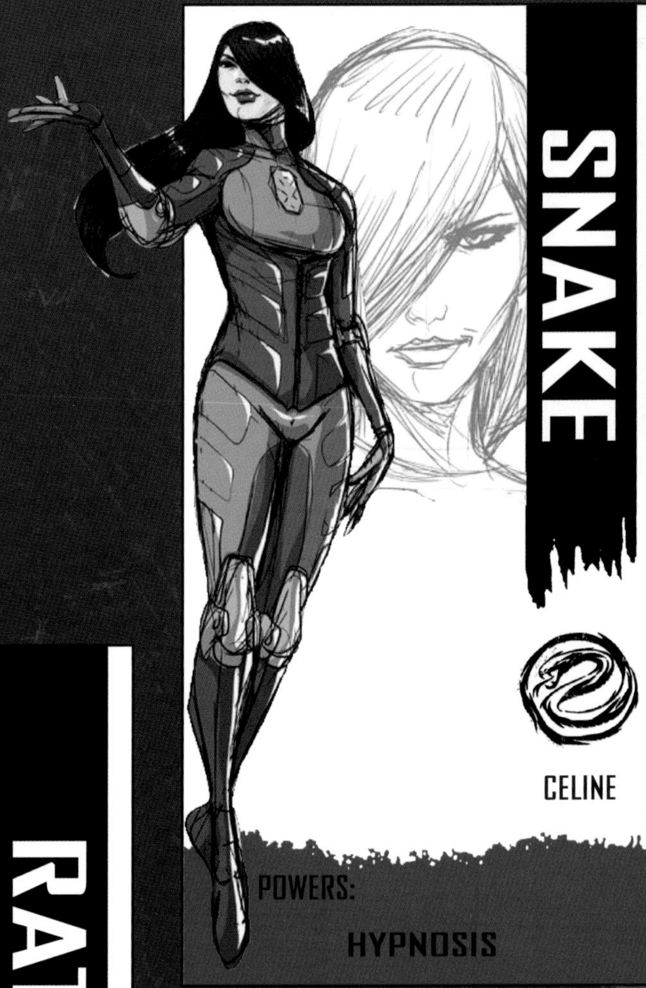
SNAKE
CELINE
POWERS:
HYPNOSIS

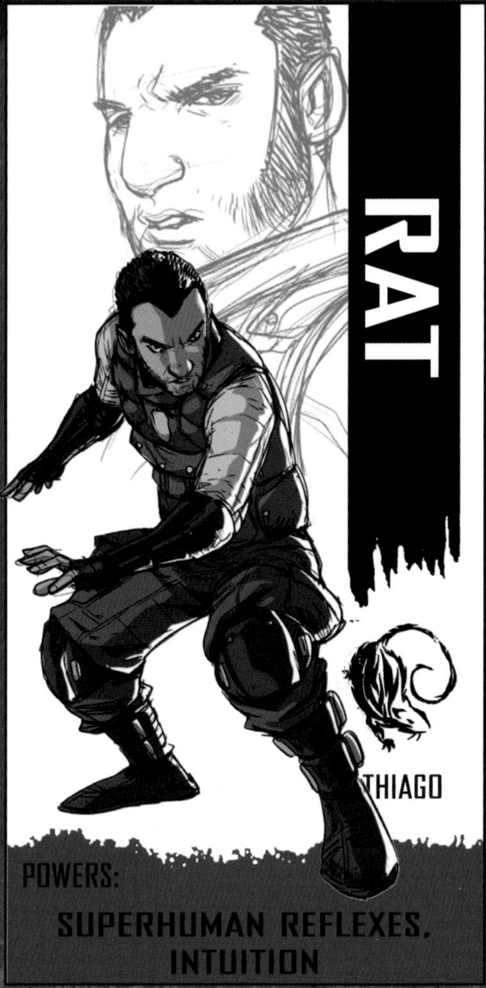
RAT
THIAGO
POWERS:
SUPERHUMAN REFLEXES, INTUITION

A timeline note: The following story takes place between the first and second novels—shortly after the end of the first book, *"The Zodiac Legacy: Convergence."*

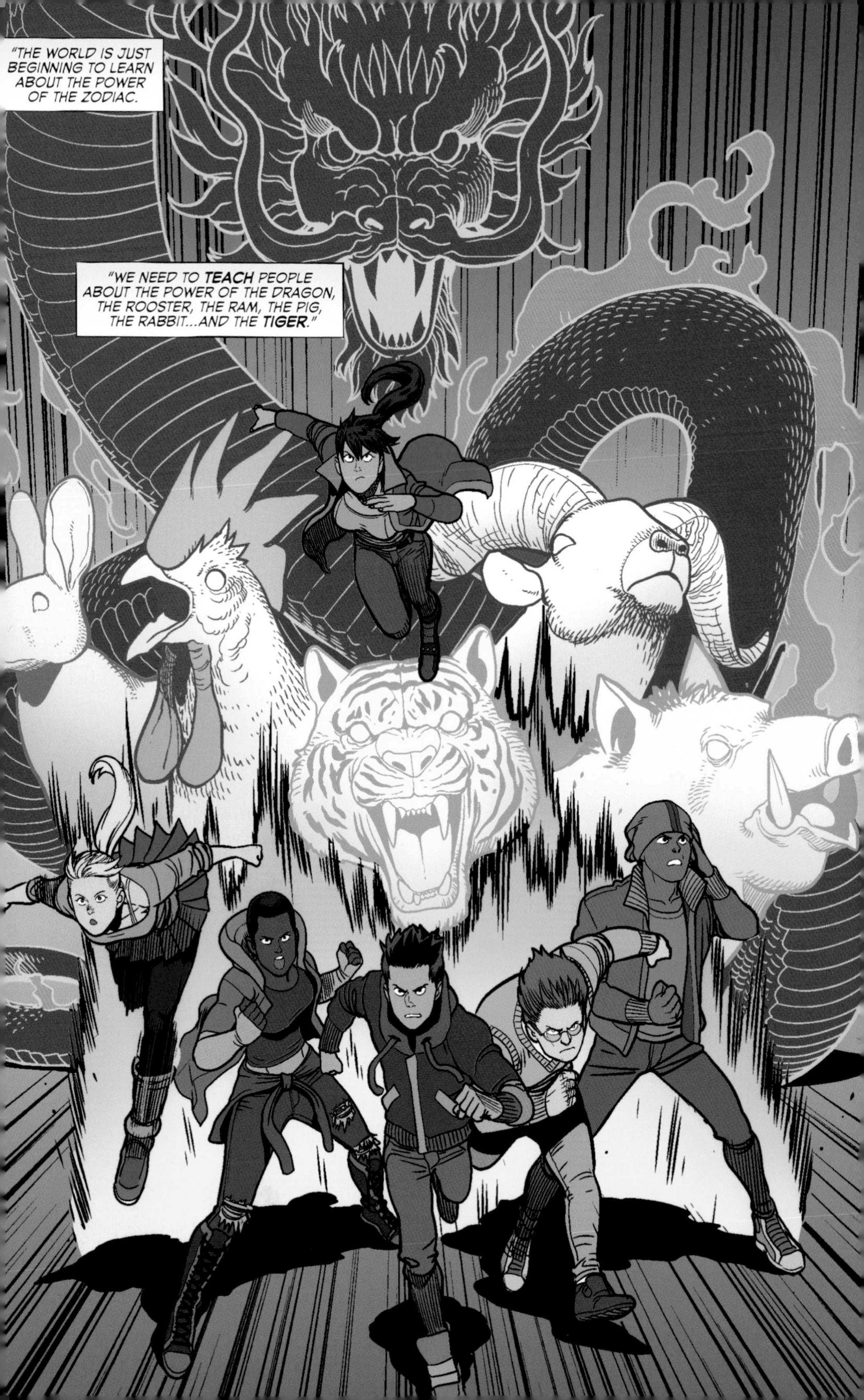
"THE WORLD IS JUST BEGINNING TO LEARN ABOUT THE POWER OF THE ZODIAC.
"WE NEED TO TEACH PEOPLE ABOUT THE POWER OF THE DRAGON, THE ROOSTER, THE RAM, THE PIG, THE RABBIT...AND THE TIGER."

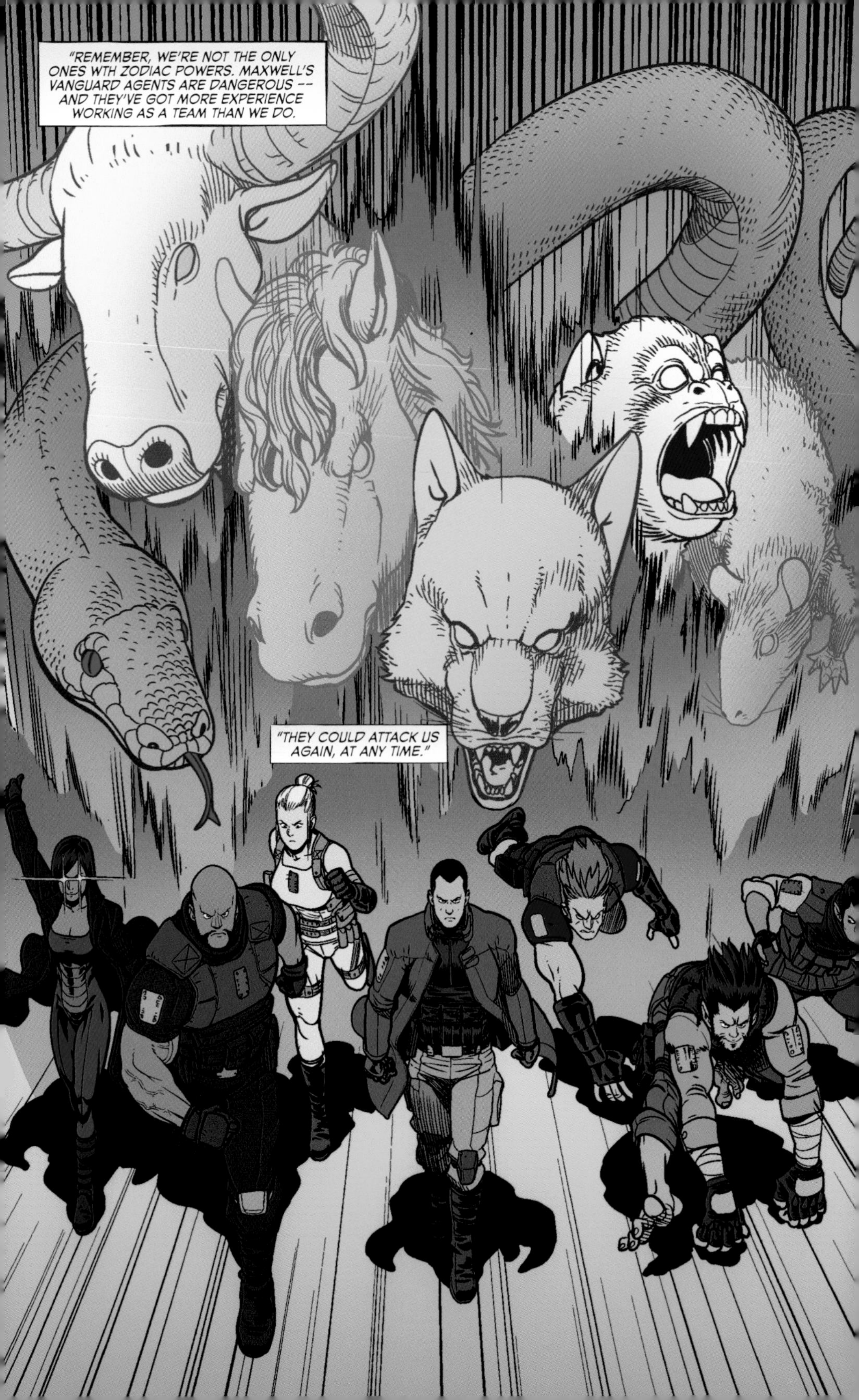
"REMEMBER, WE'RE NOT THE ONLY ONES WTH ZODIAC POWERS. MAXWELL'S VANGUARD AGENTS ARE DANGEROUS -- AND THEY'VE GOT MORE EXPERIENCE WORKING AS A TEAM THAN WE DO.
"THEY COULD ATTACK US AGAIN, AT ANY TIME."

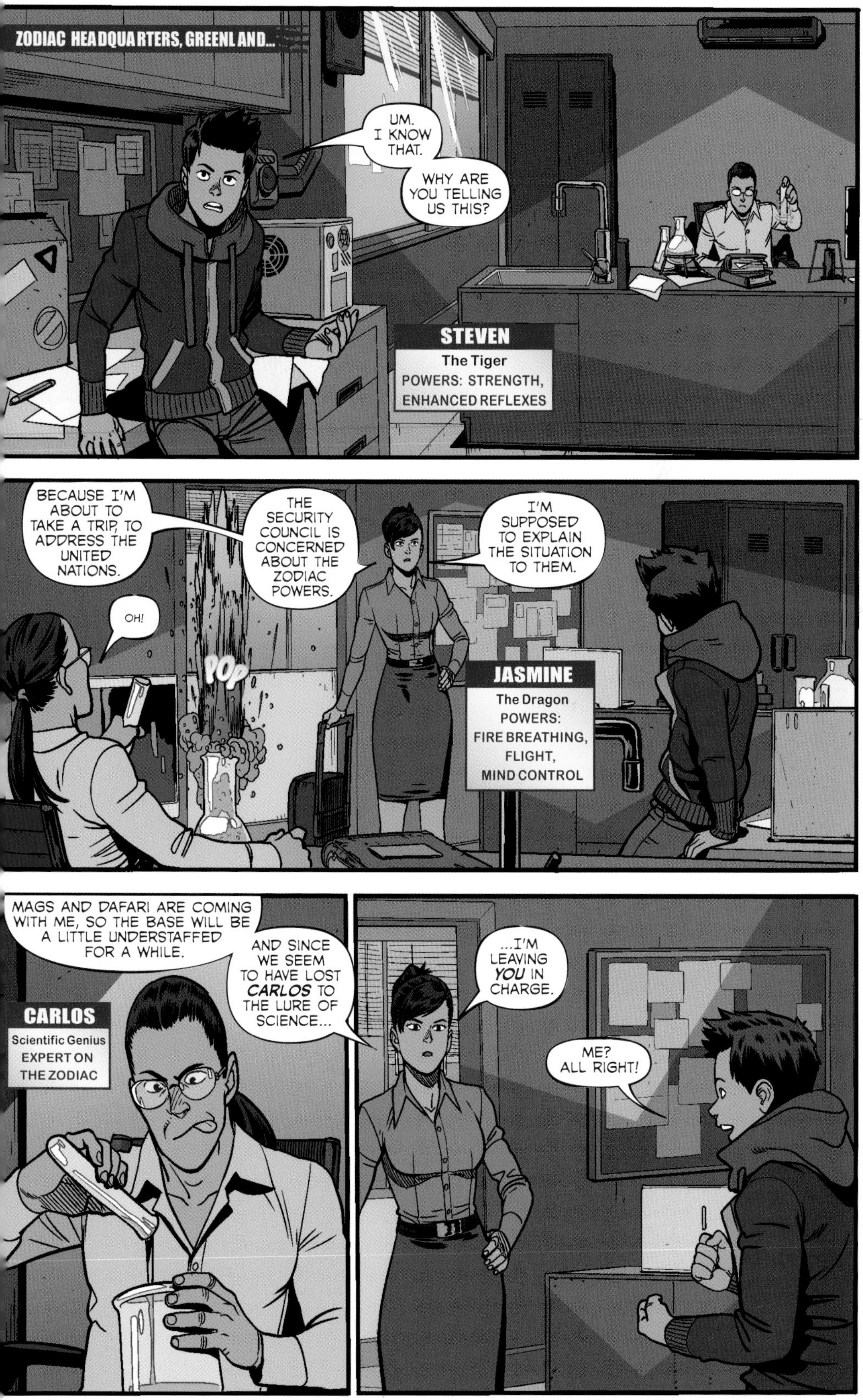
ZODIAC HEADQUARTERS, GREENLAND...
UM. I KNOW THAT.
WHY ARE YOU TELLING US THIS?
STEVEN
The Tiger
POWERS: STRENGTH, ENHANCED REFLEXES
BECAUSE I'M ABOUT TO TAKE A TRIP, TO ADDRESS THE UNITED NATIONS.
THE SECURITY COUNCIL IS CONCERNED ABOUT THE ZODIAC POWERS.
I'M SUPPOSED TO EXPLAIN THE SITUATION TO THEM.
OH!
POP
JASMINE
The Dragon
POWERS: FIRE BREATHING, FLIGHT, MIND CONTROL
MAGS AND DAFARI ARE COMING WITH ME, SO THE BASE WILL BE A LITTLE UNDERSTAFFED FOR A WHILE.
AND SINCE WE SEEM TO HAVE LOST *CARLOS* TO THE LURE OF SCIENCE...
CARLOS
Scientific Genius
EXPERT ON THE ZODIAC
...I'M LEAVING *YOU* IN CHARGE.
ME? ALL RIGHT!

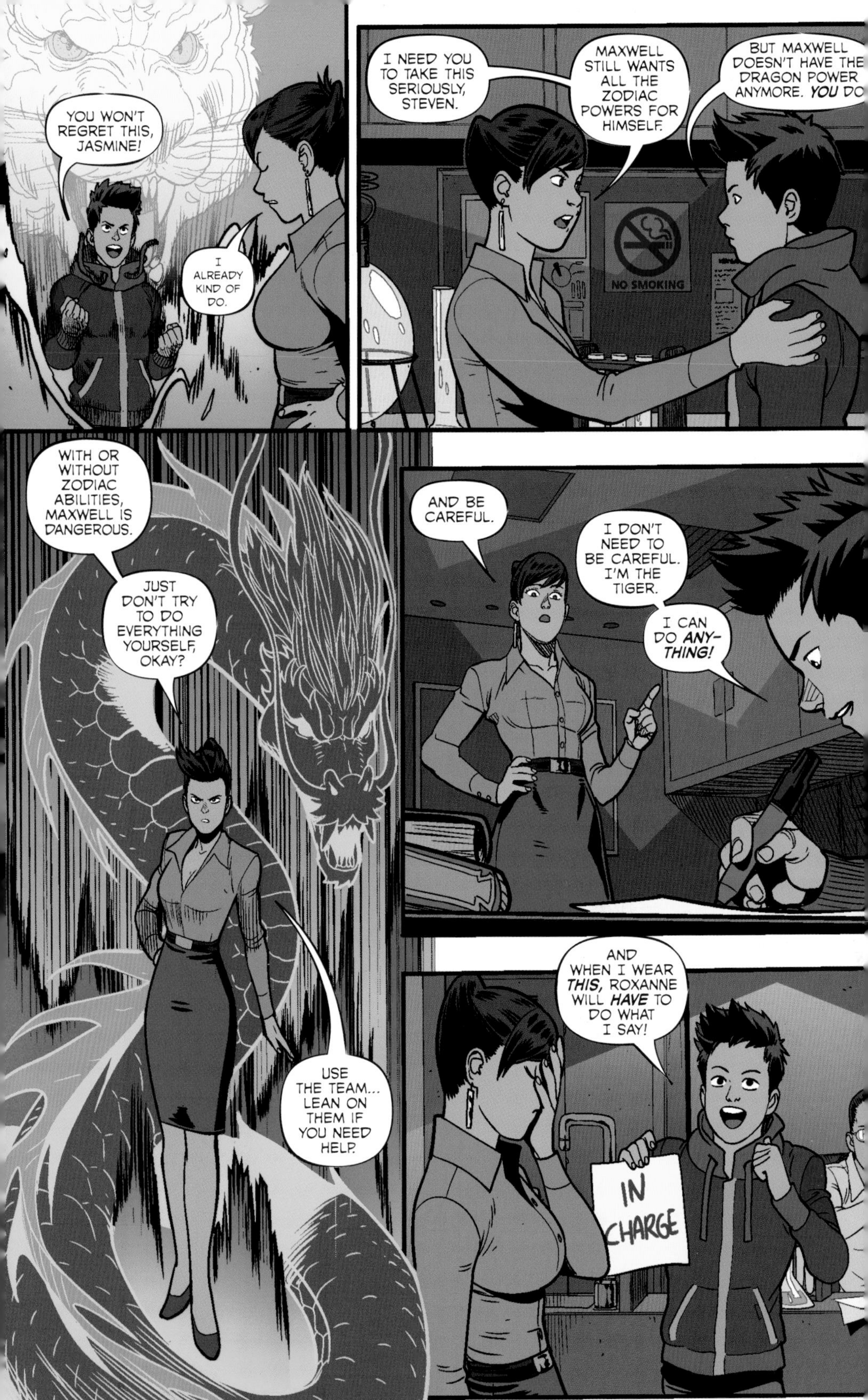
YOU WON'T REGRET THIS, JASMINE!
I ALREADY KIND OF DO.
I NEED YOU TO TAKE THIS SERIOUSLY, STEVEN.
MAXWELL STILL WANTS ALL THE ZODIAC POWERS FOR HIMSELF.
BUT MAXWELL DOESN'T HAVE THE DRAGON POWER ANYMORE. YOU DO
NO SMOKING
WITH OR WITHOUT ZODIAC ABILITIES, MAXWELL IS DANGEROUS.
JUST DON'T TRY TO DO EVERYTHING YOURSELF, OKAY?
USE THE TEAM... LEAN ON THEM IF YOU NEED HELP.
AND BE CAREFUL.
I DON'T NEED TO BE CAREFUL. I'M THE TIGER.
I CAN DO ANY-THING!
AND WHEN I WEAR THIS, ROXANNE WILL HAVE TO DO WHAT I SAY!
IN CHARGE

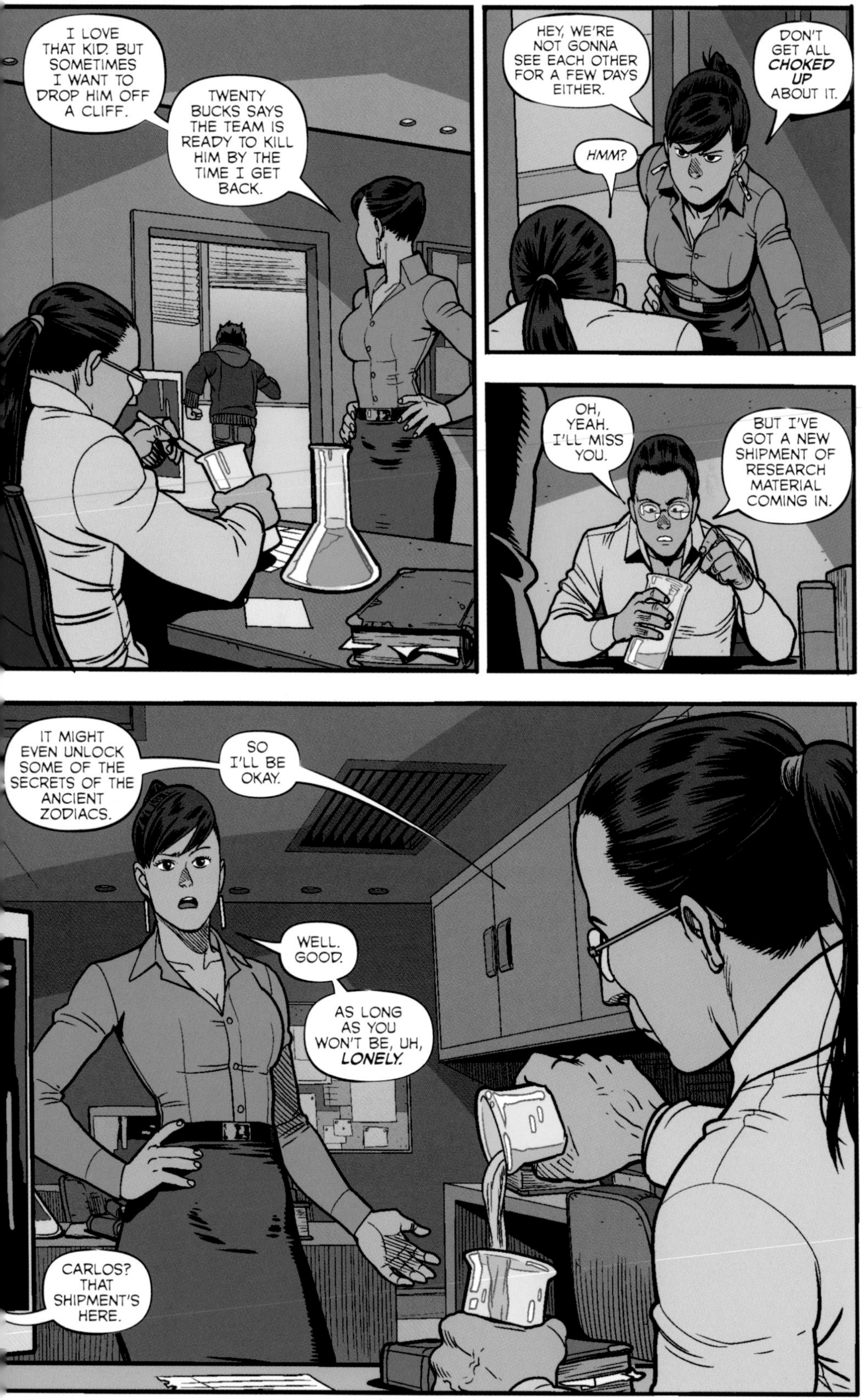
I LOVE THAT KID. BUT SOMETIMES I WANT TO DROP HIM OFF A CLIFF.
TWENTY BUCKS SAYS THE TEAM IS READY TO KILL HIM BY THE TIME I GET BACK.
HEY, WE'RE NOT GONNA SEE EACH OTHER FOR A FEW DAYS EITHER.
HMM?
DON'T GET ALL CHOKED UP ABOUT IT.
OH, YEAH. I'LL MISS YOU.
BUT I'VE GOT A NEW SHIPMENT OF RESEARCH MATERIAL COMING IN.
IT MIGHT EVEN UNLOCK SOME OF THE SECRETS OF THE ANCIENT ZODIACS.
SO I'LL BE OKAY.
WELL. GOOD.
AS LONG AS YOU WON'T BE, UH, LONELY.
CARLOS? THAT SHIPMENT'S HERE.

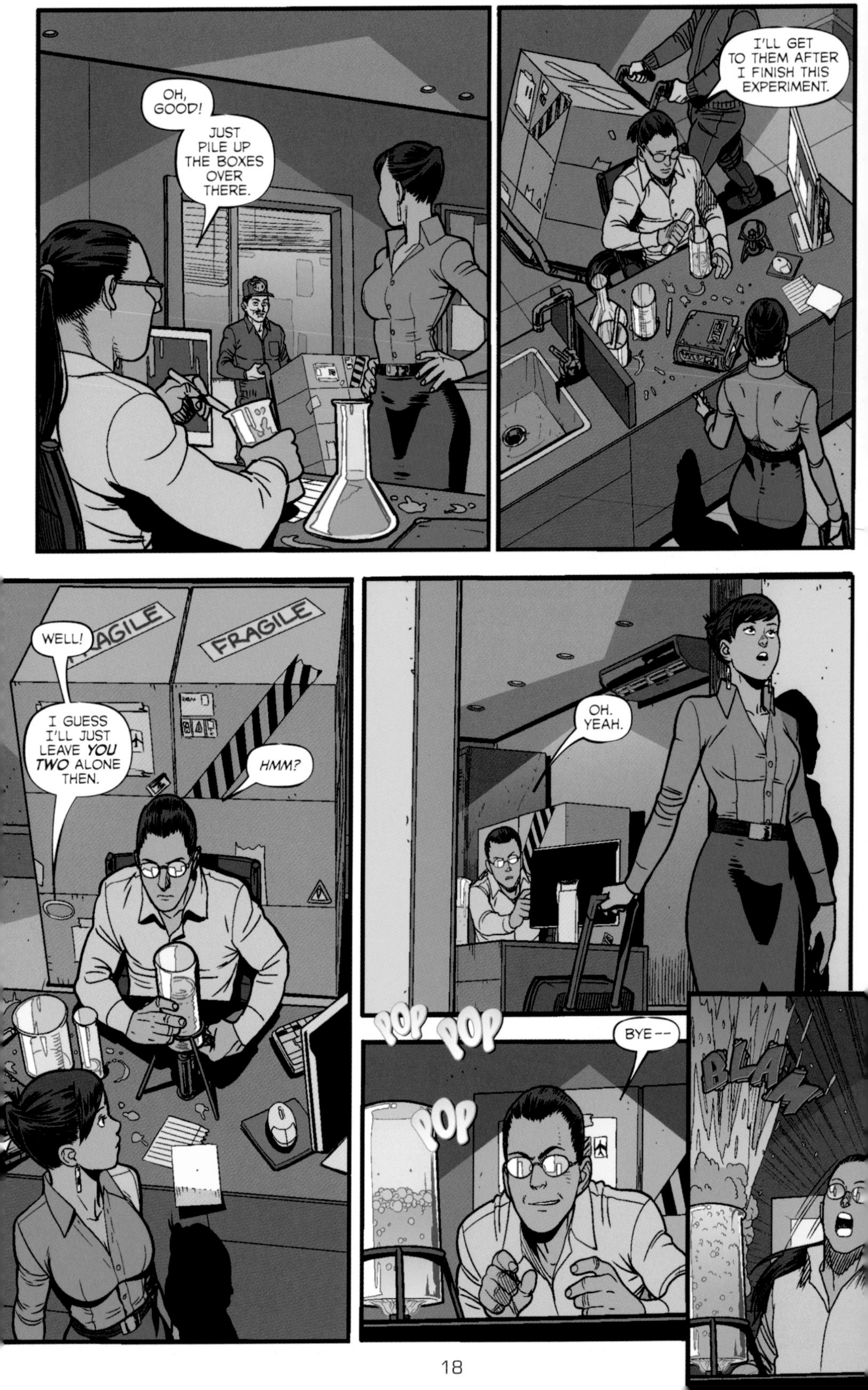
OH, GOOD!
JUST PILE UP THE BOXES OVER THERE.
I'LL GET TO THEM AFTER I FINISH THIS EXPERIMENT.
FRAGILE
FRAGILE
WELL!
I GUESS I'LL JUST LEAVE *YOU TWO* ALONE THEN.
HMM?
OH. YEAH.
POP POP
POP
BYE--
BLAM

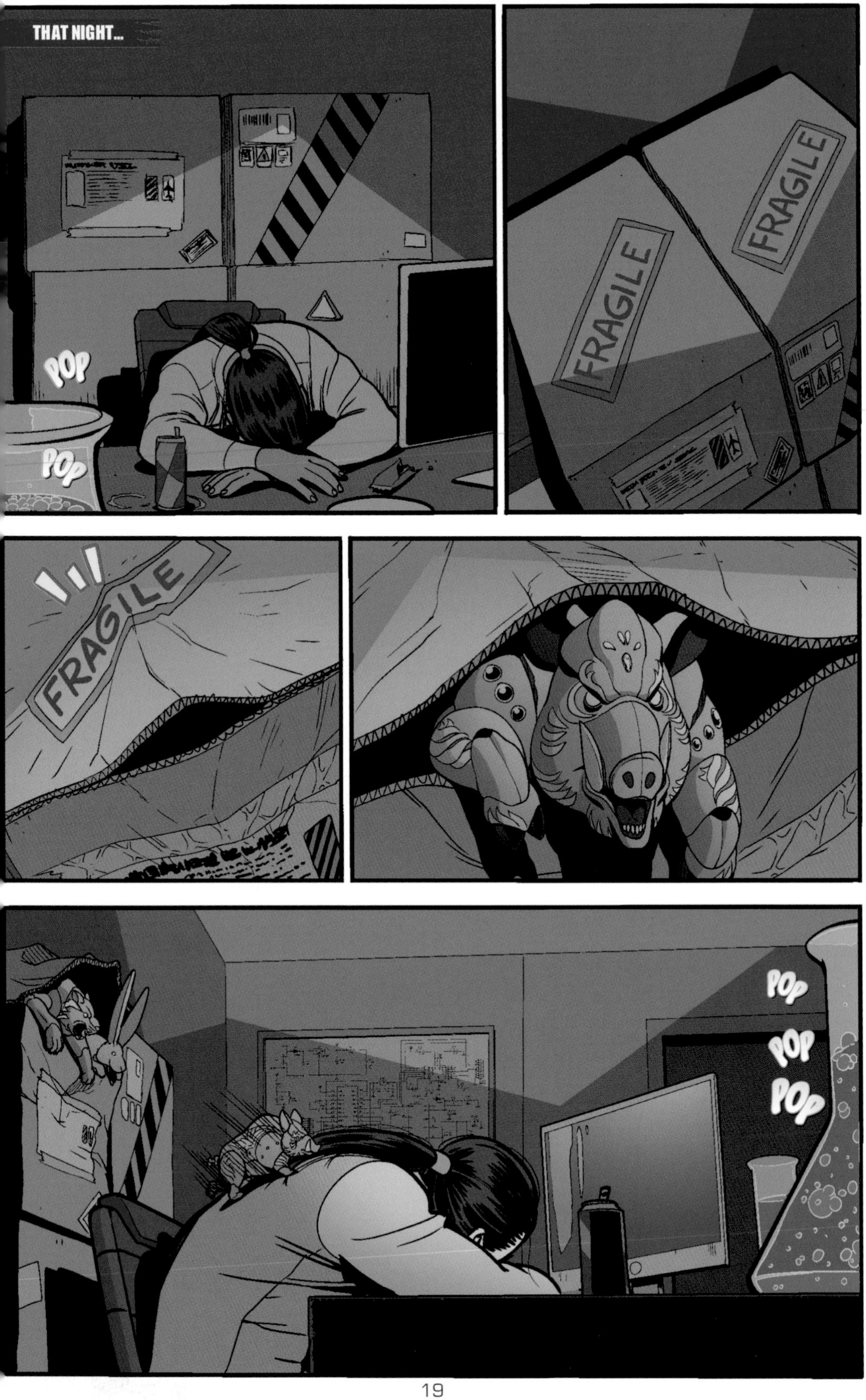
THAT NIGHT...
POP
POP
FRAGILE
FRAGILE
FRAGILE
POP
POP
POP

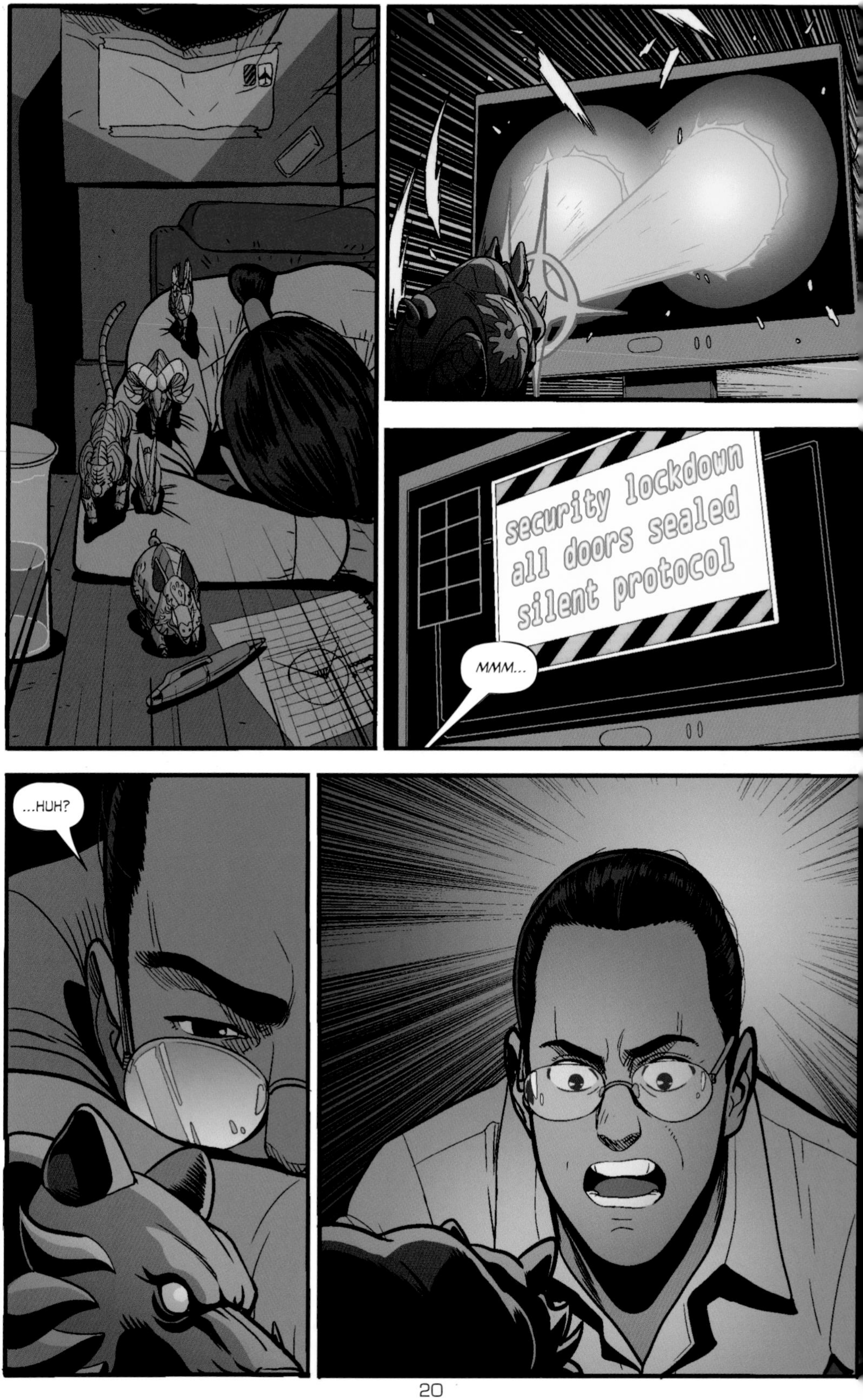
security lockdown
all doors sealed
silent protocol
MMM...
...HUH?

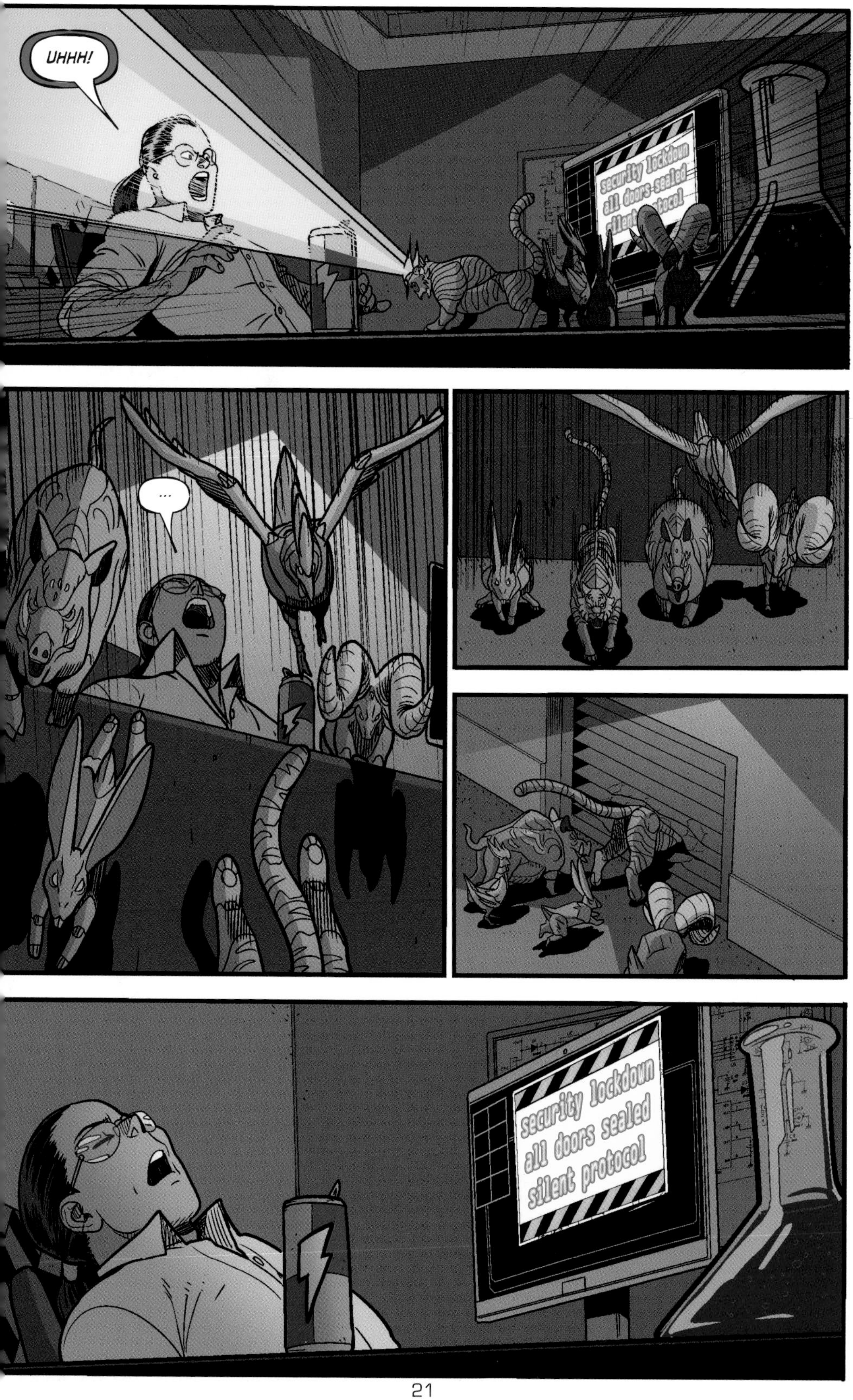
UHHH!
security lockdown
all doors-sealed
...
security lockdown
all doors sealed
silent protocol

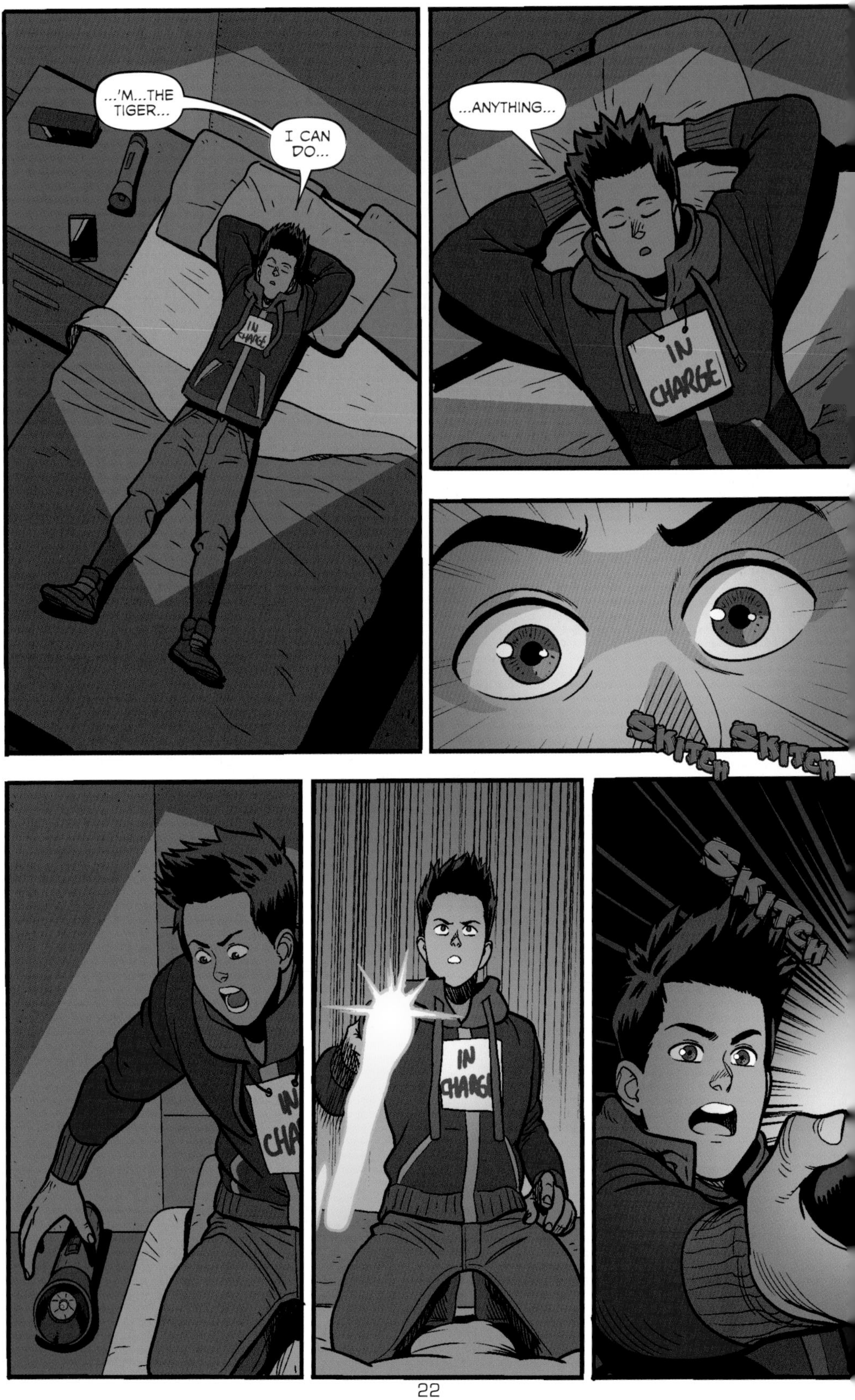
...'M...THE TIGER...
I CAN DO...
...ANYTHING...
IN CHARGE
IN CHARGE
SKITCH SKITCH
IN CHARGE
SKITCH

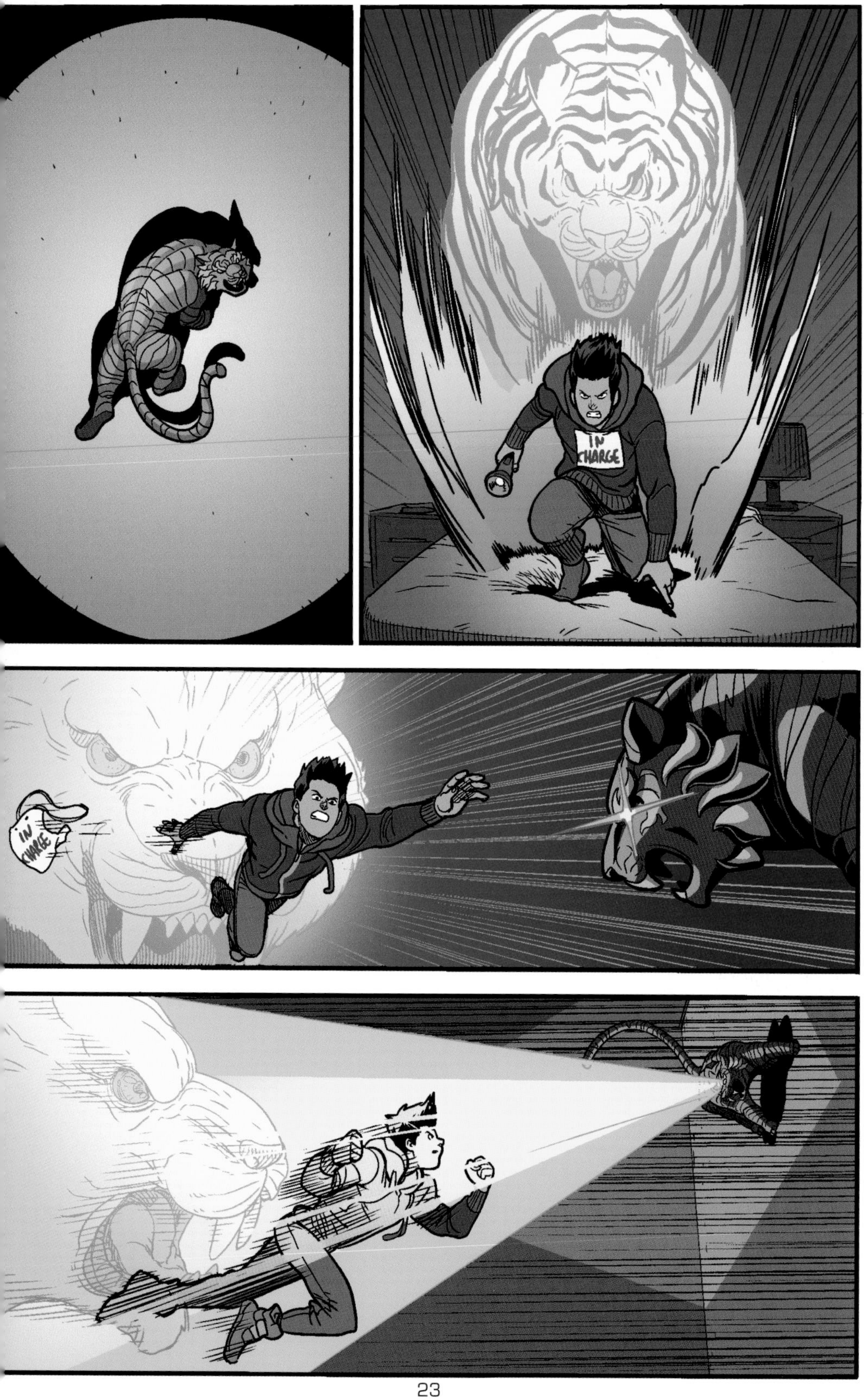
IN CHARGE
IN CHARGE

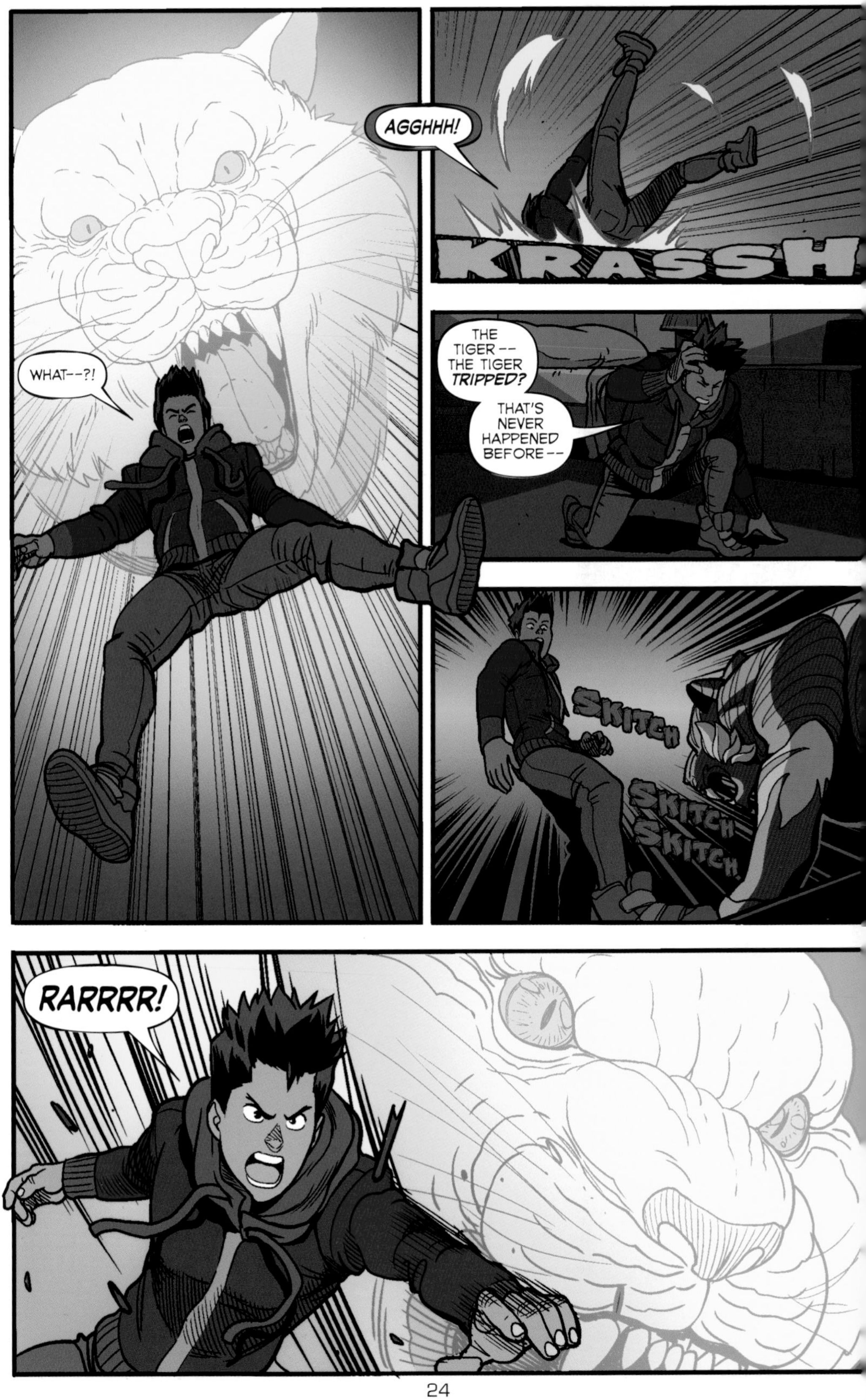
WHAT--?!
AGGHHH!
KRASSH
THE TIGER -- THE TIGER TRIPPED?
THAT'S NEVER HAPPENED BEFORE --
SKITCH
SKITCH
SKITCH
RARRRR!

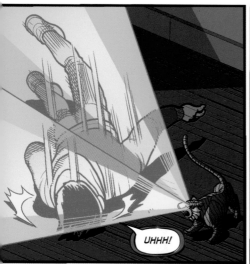

UHHH!

WHATEVER THAT THING IS, IT'S *NEUTRALIZING* MY ZODIAC POWER.

INTERFERING WITH THE TIGER'S AGILITY, ITS FIGHTING INSTINCTS.

WITHOUT THAT, I'M *HELPLESS!*

WE'RE-- WE'RE UNDER ATTACK.

I'VE GOT TO WARN THE OTHERS--

SKITCH
SKITCH

security lockdown
all doors sealed

NGGGHH--

UHHH!

KLUNNK

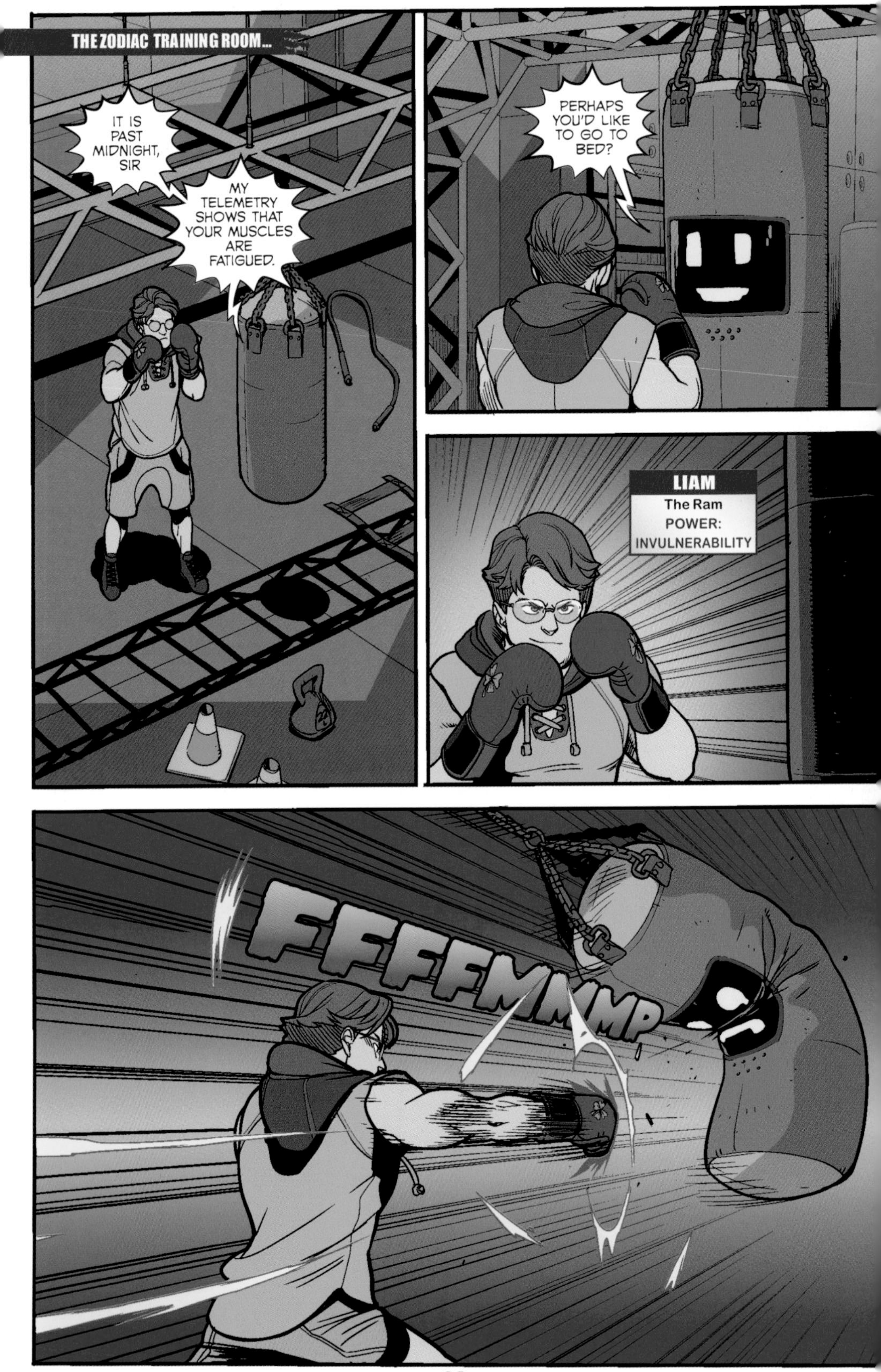
THE ZODIAC TRAINING ROOM...
IT IS PAST MIDNIGHT, SIR
MY TELEMETRY SHOWS THAT YOUR MUSCLES ARE FATIGUED.
PERHAPS YOU'D LIKE TO GO TO BED?
LIAM
The Ram
POWER: INVULNERABILITY
FFFFMMMP

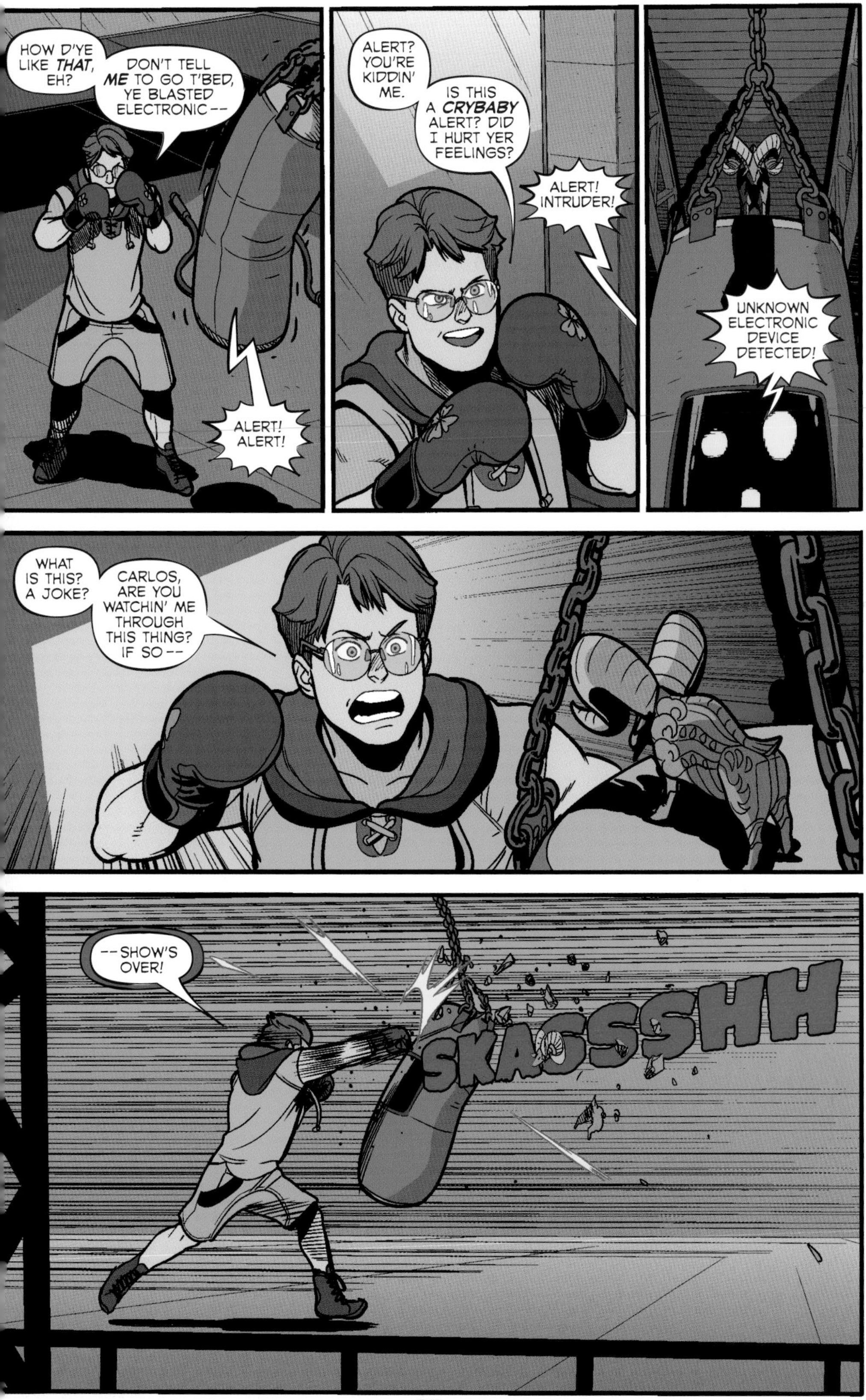
HOW D'YE LIKE *THAT*, EH?
DON'T TELL *ME* TO GO T'BED, YE BLASTED ELECTRONIC--
ALERT! ALERT!
ALERT? YOU'RE KIDDIN' ME.
IS THIS A *CRYBABY* ALERT? DID I HURT YER FEELINGS?
ALERT! INTRUDER!
UNKNOWN ELECTRONIC DEVICE DETECTED!
WHAT IS THIS? A JOKE?
CARLOS, ARE YOU WATCHIN' ME THROUGH THIS THING? IF SO--
--SHOW'S OVER!
SKASSSHH

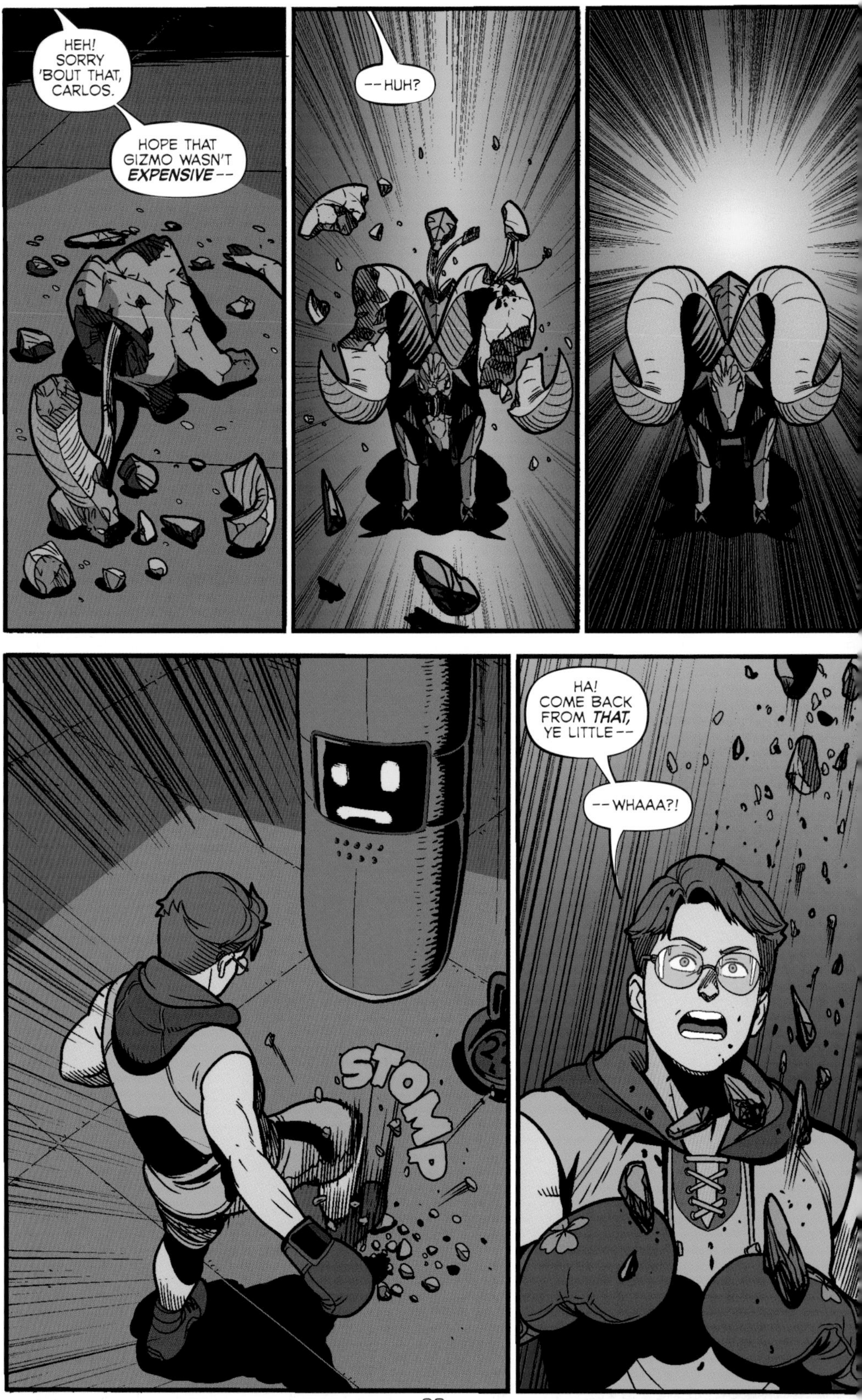
HEH! SORRY 'BOUT THAT, CARLOS.
HOPE THAT GIZMO WASN'T *EXPENSIVE*--
--HUH?
STOMP
HA! COME BACK FROM *THAT,* YE LITTLE--
--WHAAA?!

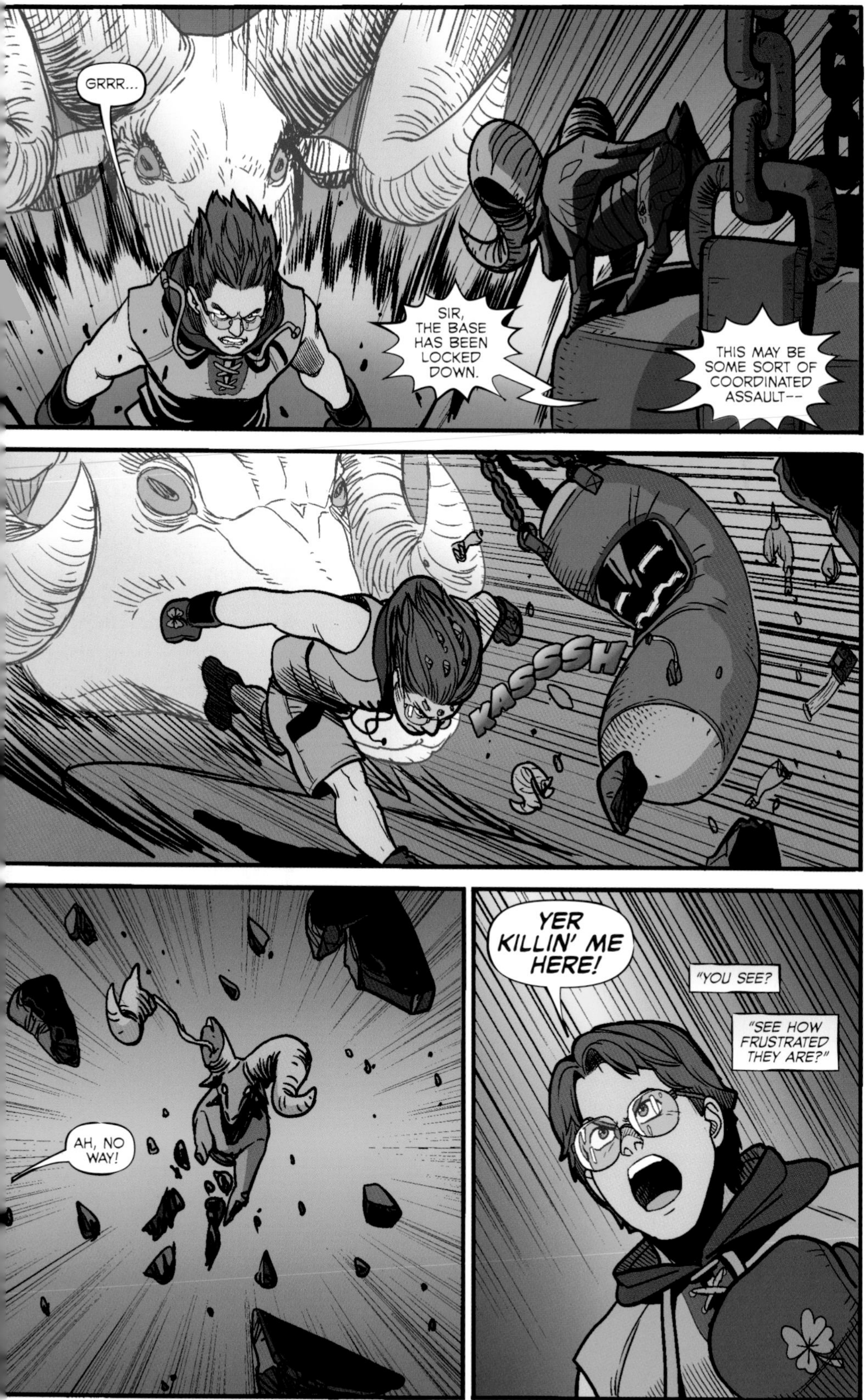
GRRR...
SIR, THE BASE HAS BEEN LOCKED DOWN.
THIS MAY BE SOME SORT OF COORDINATED ASSAULT--
KASSSH
AH, NO WAY!
YER KILLIN' ME HERE!
"YOU SEE?
"SEE HOW FRUSTRATED THEY ARE?"

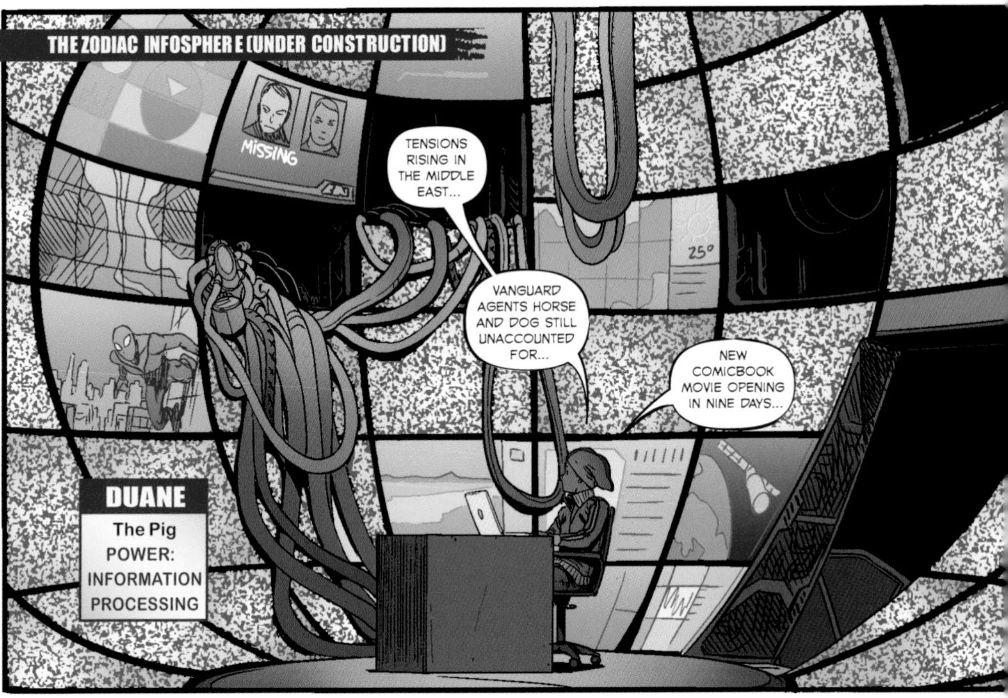
THE ZODIAC INFOSPHERE (UNDER CONSTRUCTION)
MISSING
TENSIONS RISING IN THE MIDDLE EAST...
VANGUARD AGENTS HORSE AND DOG STILL UNACCOUNTED FOR...
NEW COMICBOOK MOVIE OPENING IN NINE DAYS...
25°
DUANE
The Pig
POWER:
INFORMATION PROCESSING

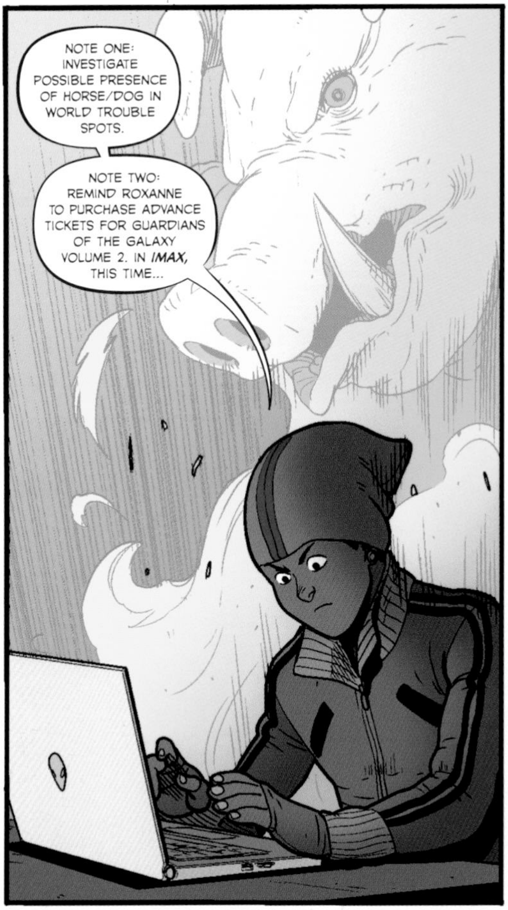
NOTE ONE: INVESTIGATE POSSIBLE PRESENCE OF HORSE/DOG IN WORLD TROUBLE SPOTS.
NOTE TWO: REMIND ROXANNE TO PURCHASE ADVANCE TICKETS FOR GUARDIANS OF THE GALAXY VOLUME 2. IN *IMAX,* THIS TIME...

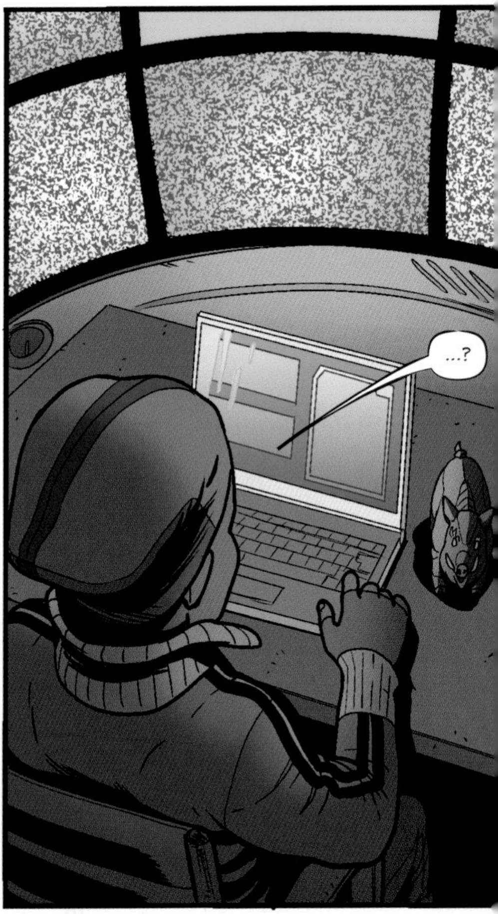
...?

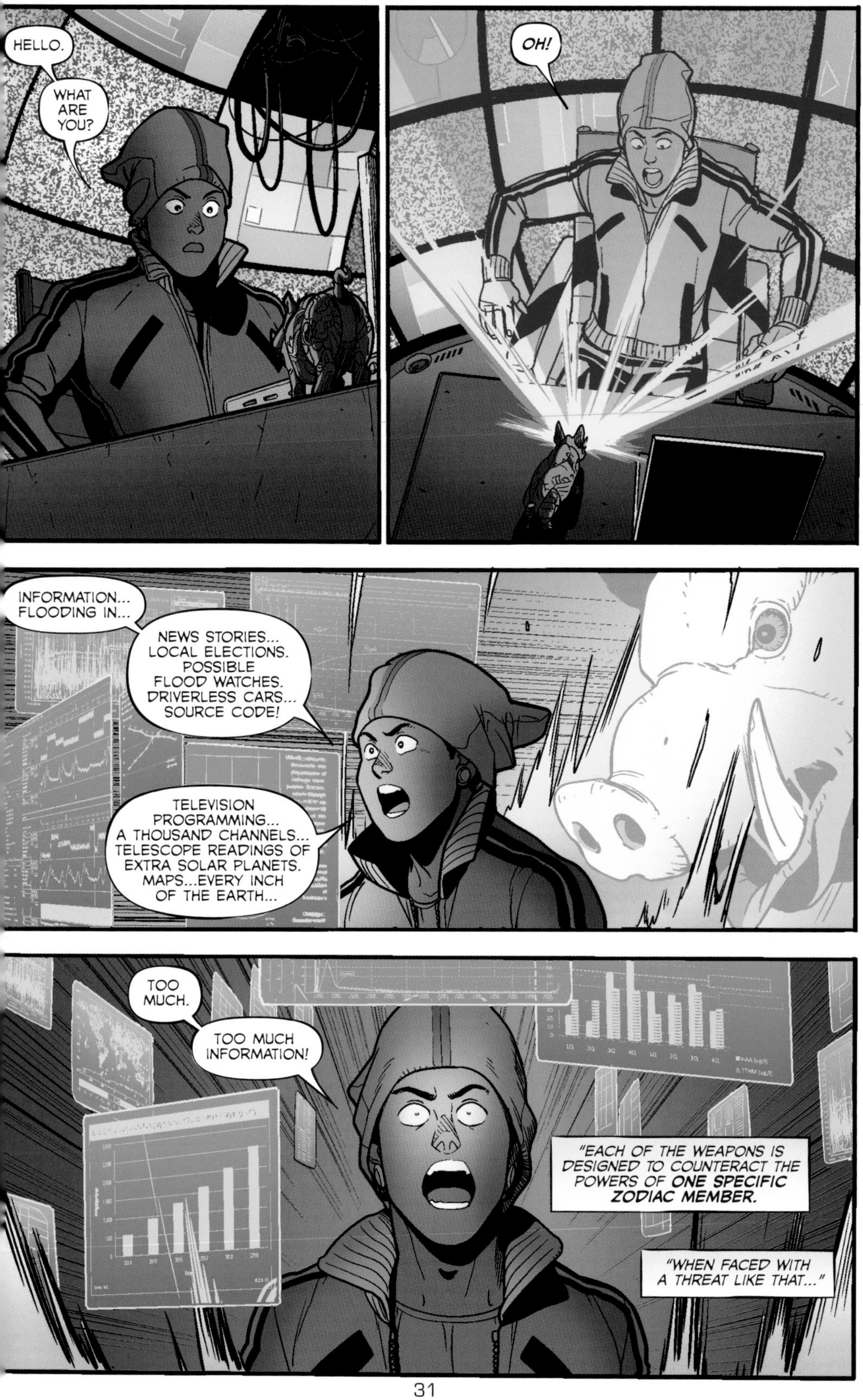
HELLO.
WHAT ARE YOU?
OH!
INFORMATION... FLOODING IN...
NEWS STORIES... LOCAL ELECTIONS. POSSIBLE FLOOD WATCHES. DRIVERLESS CARS... SOURCE CODE!
TELEVISION PROGRAMMING... A THOUSAND CHANNELS... TELESCOPE READINGS OF EXTRA SOLAR PLANETS. MAPS...EVERY INCH OF THE EARTH...
TOO MUCH.
TOO MUCH INFORMATION!
"EACH OF THE WEAPONS IS DESIGNED TO COUNTERACT THE POWERS OF **ONE SPECIFIC ZODIAC MEMBER.**
"WHEN FACED WITH A THREAT LIKE THAT..."

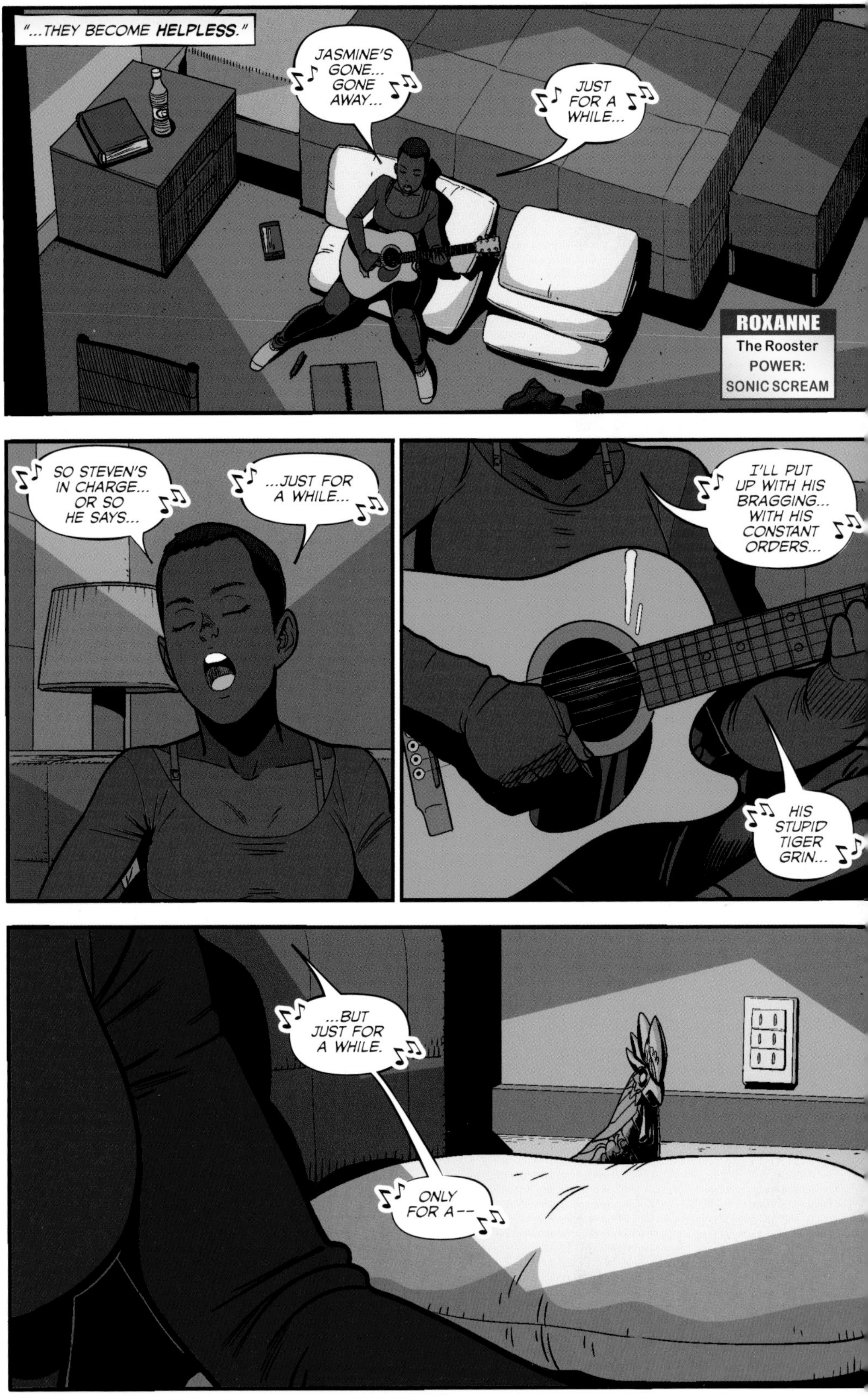
"...THEY BECOME **HELPLESS.**"
JASMINE'S GONE... GONE AWAY...
JUST FOR A WHILE...
ROXANNE
The Rooster
POWER:
SONIC SCREAM
SO STEVEN'S IN CHARGE... OR SO HE SAYS...
...JUST FOR A WHILE...
I'LL PUT UP WITH HIS BRAGGING... WITH HIS CONSTANT ORDERS...
HIS STUPID TIGER GRIN...
...BUT JUST FOR A WHILE.
ONLY FOR A--

-- FOR A --

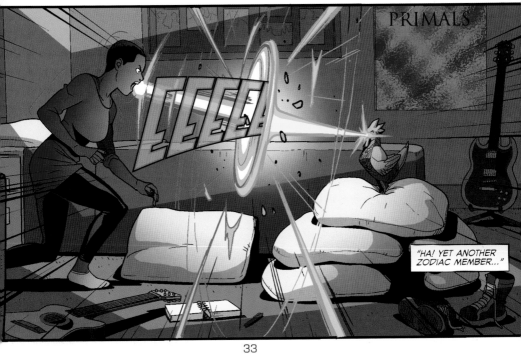

PRIMALS

"HA! YET ANOTHER ZODIAC MEMBER..."

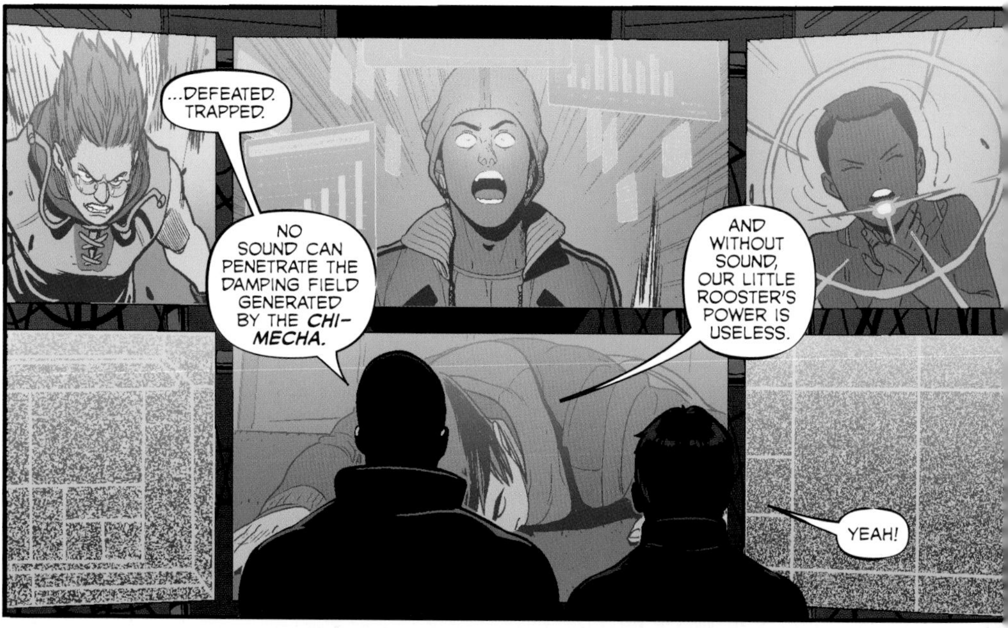
...DEFEATED. TRAPPED.
NO SOUND CAN PENETRATE THE DAMPING FIELD GENERATED BY THE CHI-MECHA.
AND WITHOUT SOUND, OUR LITTLE ROOSTER'S POWER IS USELESS.
YEAH!

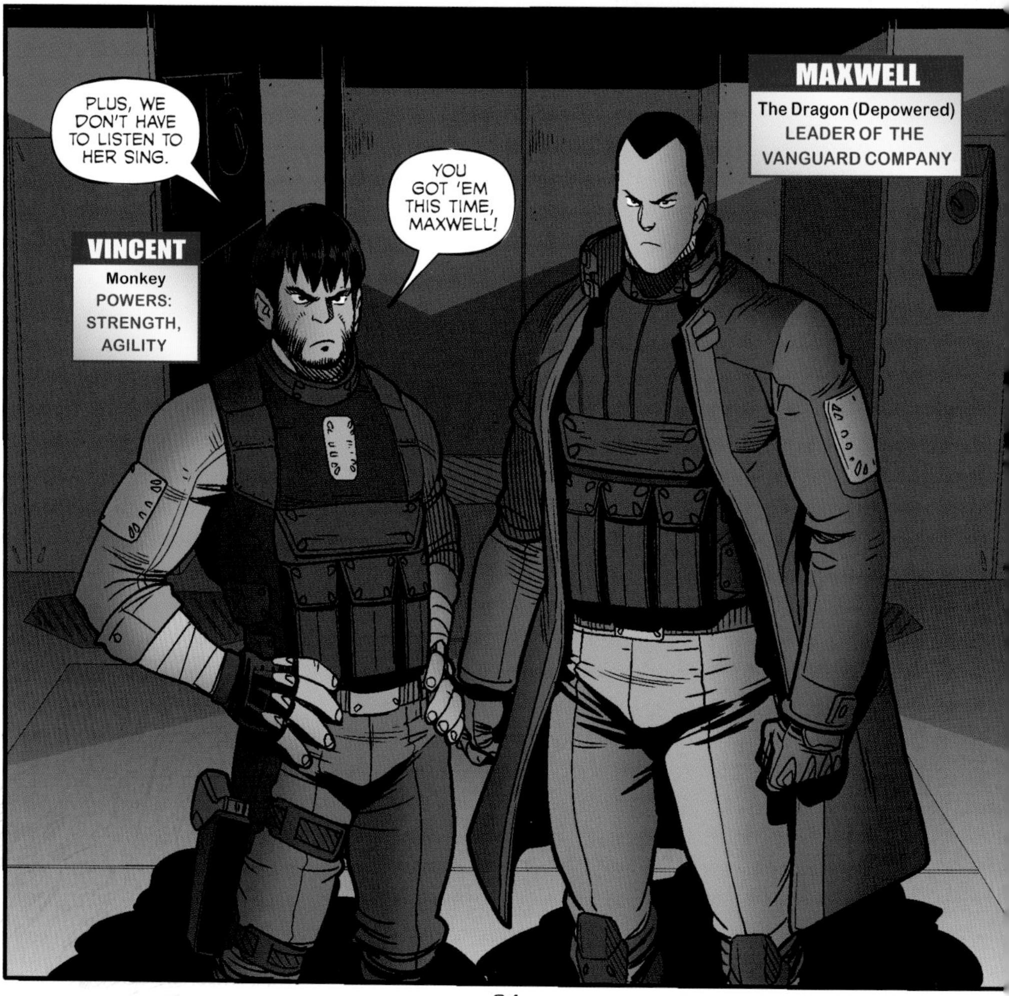
MAXWELL
The Dragon (Depowered)
LEADER OF THE VANGUARD COMPANY
PLUS, WE DON'T HAVE TO LISTEN TO HER SING.
YOU GOT 'EM THIS TIME, MAXWELL!
VINCENT
Monkey
POWERS: STRENGTH, AGILITY

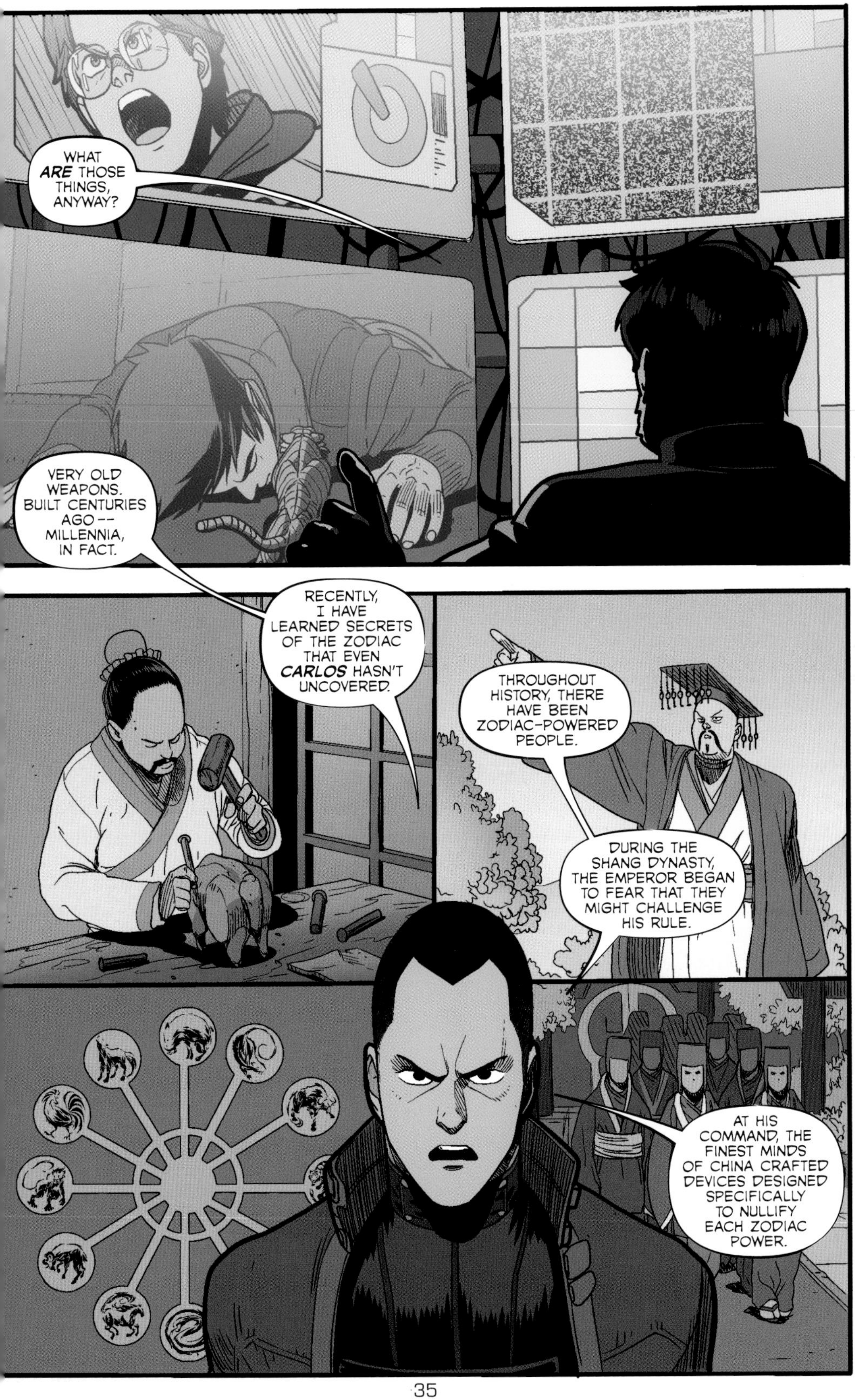
WHAT ARE THOSE THINGS, ANYWAY?
VERY OLD WEAPONS. BUILT CENTURIES AGO-- MILLENNIA, IN FACT.
RECENTLY, I HAVE LEARNED SECRETS OF THE ZODIAC THAT EVEN CARLOS HASN'T UNCOVERED.
THROUGHOUT HISTORY, THERE HAVE BEEN ZODIAC-POWERED PEOPLE.
DURING THE SHANG DYNASTY, THE EMPEROR BEGAN TO FEAR THAT THEY MIGHT CHALLENGE HIS RULE.
AT HIS COMMAND, THE FINEST MINDS OF CHINA CRAFTED DEVICES DESIGNED SPECIFICALLY TO NULLIFY EACH ZODIAC POWER.

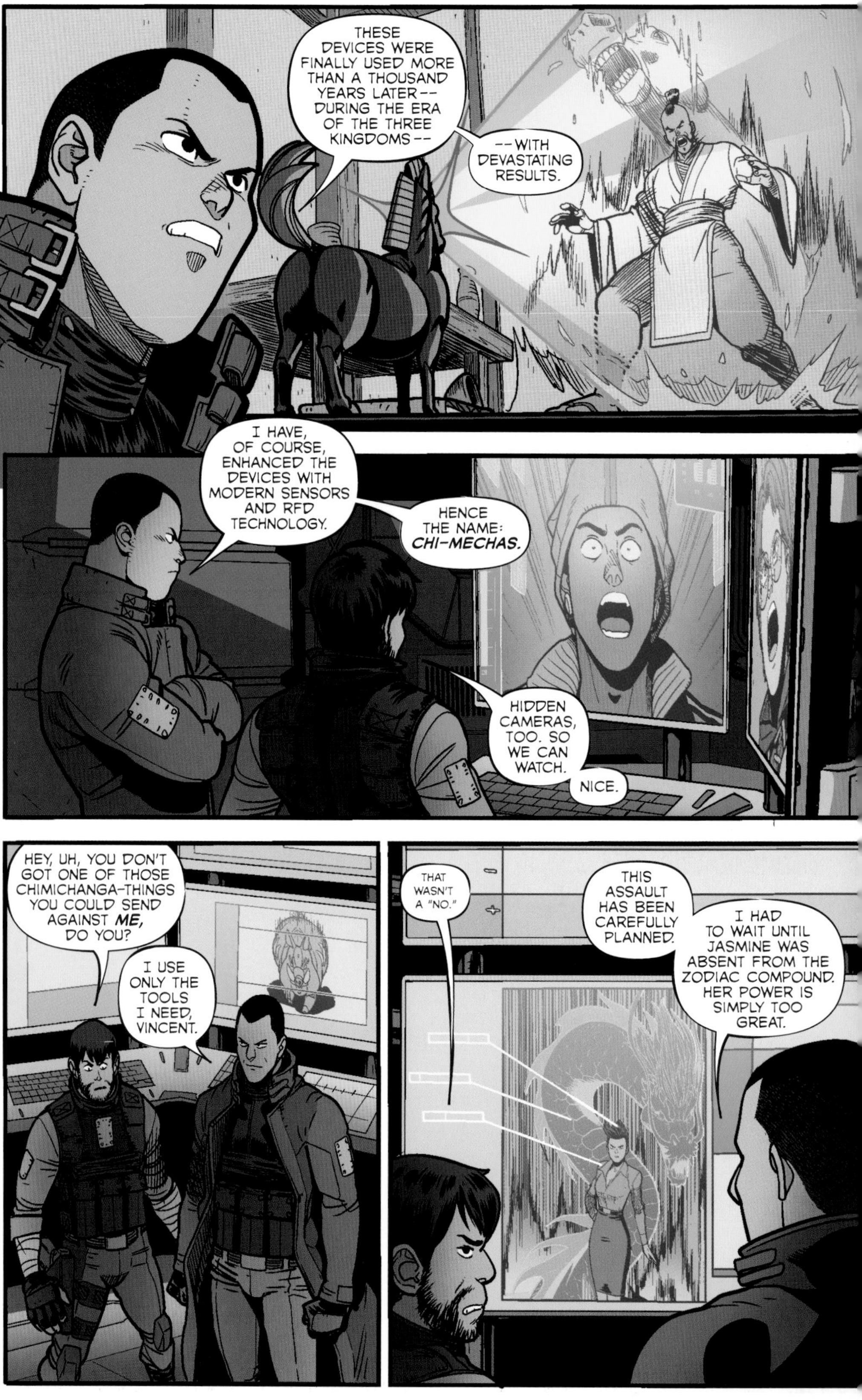
THESE DEVICES WERE FINALLY USED MORE THAN A THOUSAND YEARS LATER-- DURING THE ERA OF THE THREE KINGDOMS--
--WITH DEVASTATING RESULTS.
I HAVE, OF COURSE, ENHANCED THE DEVICES WITH MODERN SENSORS AND RFD TECHNOLOGY.
HENCE THE NAME: CHI-MECHAS.
HIDDEN CAMERAS, TOO. SO WE CAN WATCH.
NICE.
HEY, UH, YOU DON'T GOT ONE OF THOSE CHIMICHANGA-THINGS YOU COULD SEND AGAINST ME, DO YOU?
I USE ONLY THE TOOLS I NEED, VINCENT.
THAT WASN'T A "NO."
THIS ASSAULT HAS BEEN CAREFULLY PLANNED.
I HAD TO WAIT UNTIL JASMINE WAS ABSENT FROM THE ZODIAC COMPOUND. HER POWER IS SIMPLY TOO GREAT.

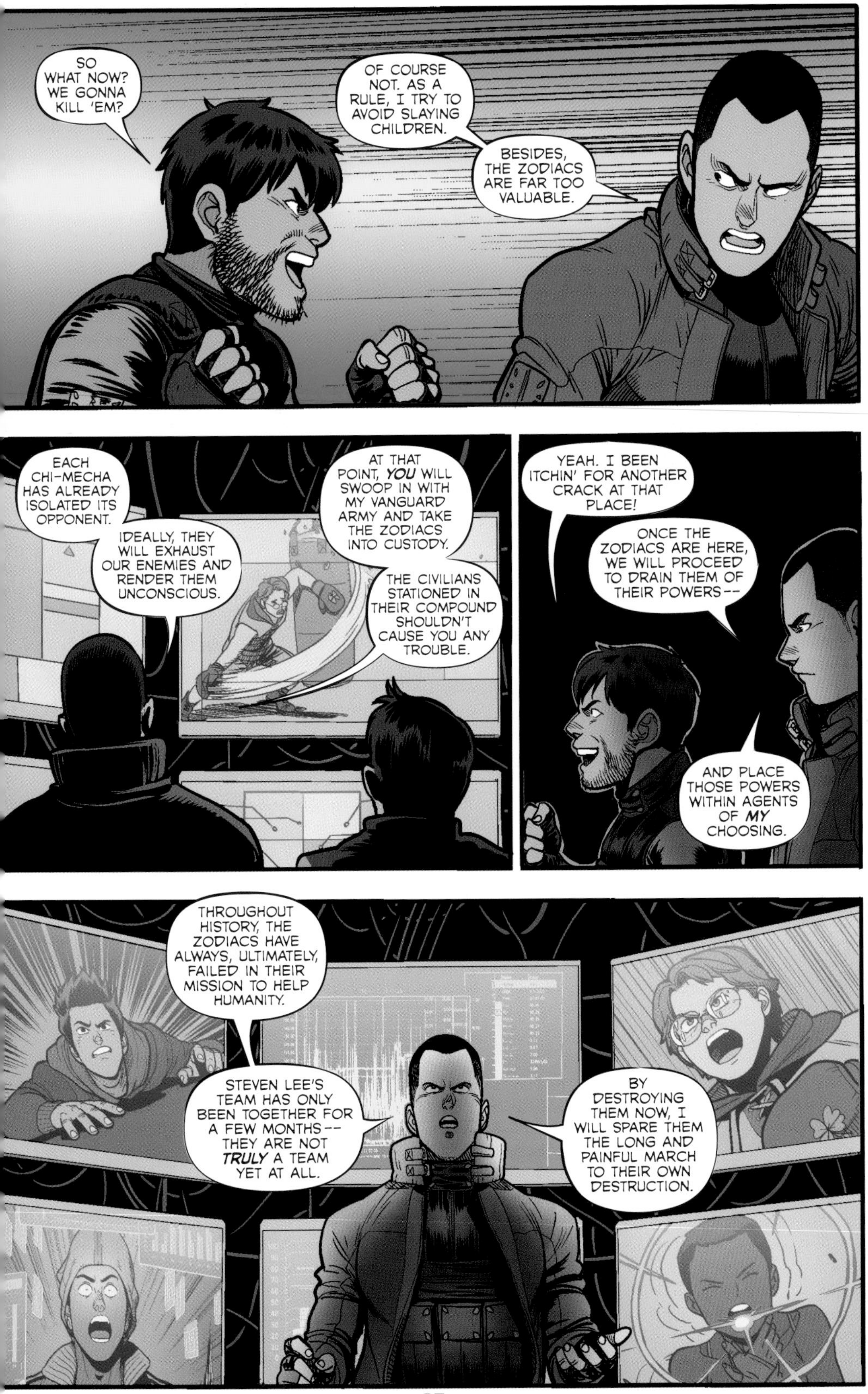

SO WHAT NOW? WE GONNA KILL 'EM?
OF COURSE NOT. AS A RULE, I TRY TO AVOID SLAYING CHILDREN.
BESIDES, THE ZODIACS ARE FAR TOO VALUABLE.
EACH CHI-MECHA HAS ALREADY ISOLATED ITS OPPONENT.
IDEALLY, THEY WILL EXHAUST OUR ENEMIES AND RENDER THEM UNCONSCIOUS.
AT THAT POINT, *YOU* WILL SWOOP IN WITH MY VANGUARD ARMY AND TAKE THE ZODIACS INTO CUSTODY.
THE CIVILIANS STATIONED IN THEIR COMPOUND SHOULDN'T CAUSE YOU ANY TROUBLE.
YEAH. I BEEN ITCHIN' FOR ANOTHER CRACK AT THAT PLACE!
ONCE THE ZODIACS ARE HERE, WE WILL PROCEED TO DRAIN THEM OF THEIR POWERS--
AND PLACE THOSE POWERS WITHIN AGENTS OF *MY* CHOOSING.
THROUGHOUT HISTORY, THE ZODIACS HAVE ALWAYS, ULTIMATELY, FAILED IN THEIR MISSION TO HELP HUMANITY.
STEVEN LEE'S TEAM HAS ONLY BEEN TOGETHER FOR A FEW MONTHS-- THEY ARE NOT *TRULY* A TEAM YET AT ALL.
BY DESTROYING THEM NOW, I WILL SPARE THEM THE LONG AND PAINFUL MARCH TO THEIR OWN DESTRUCTION.

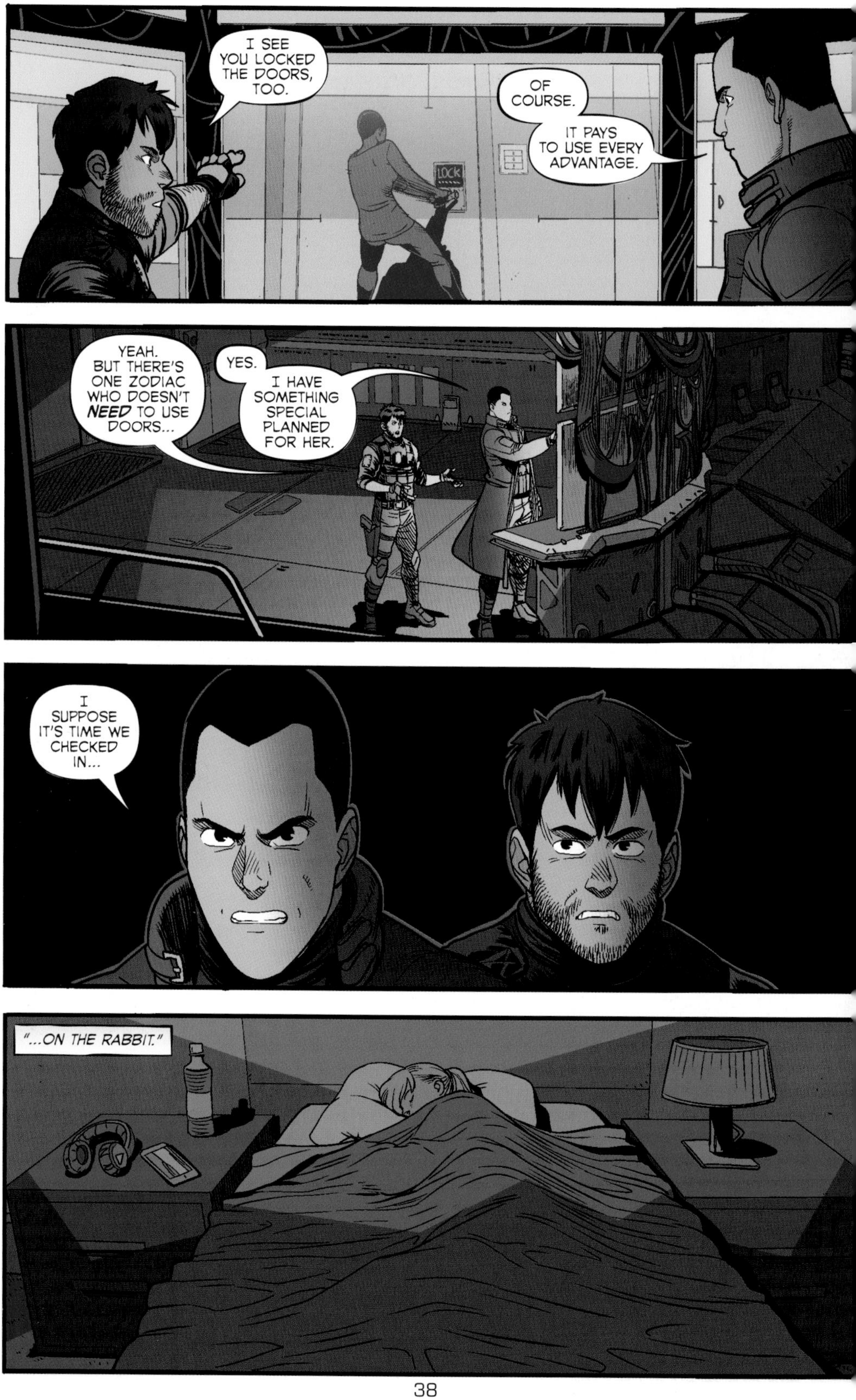
I SEE YOU LOCKED THE DOORS, TOO.
LOCK
OF COURSE.
IT PAYS TO USE EVERY ADVANTAGE.
YEAH. BUT THERE'S ONE ZODIAC WHO DOESN'T *NEED* TO USE DOORS...
YES.
I HAVE SOMETHING SPECIAL PLANNED FOR HER.
I SUPPOSE IT'S TIME WE CHECKED IN...
"...ON THE RABBIT."

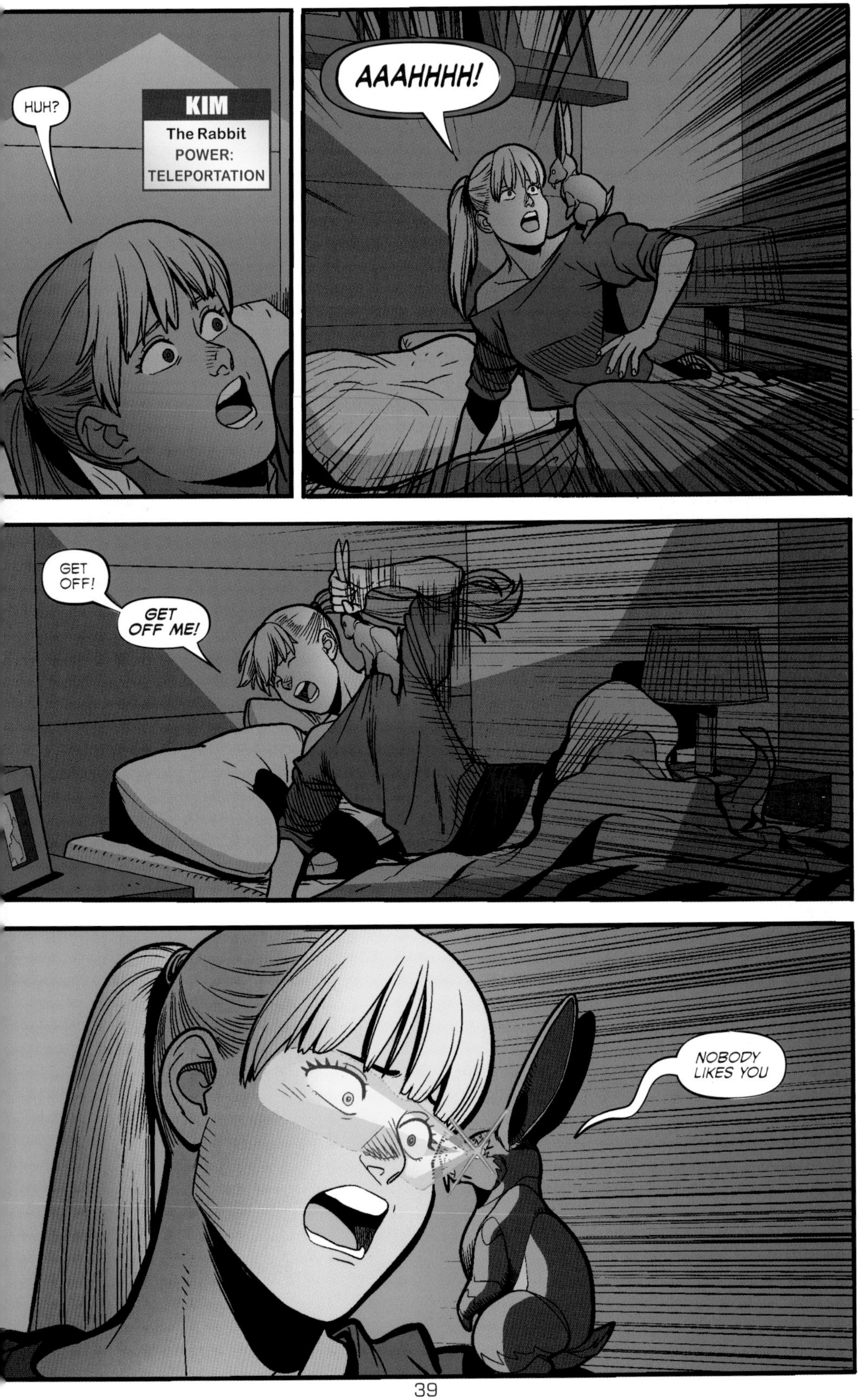
HUH?
KIM
The Rabbit
POWER:
TELEPORTATION
AAAHHHH!
GET OFF!
GET OFF ME!
NOBODY LIKES YOU

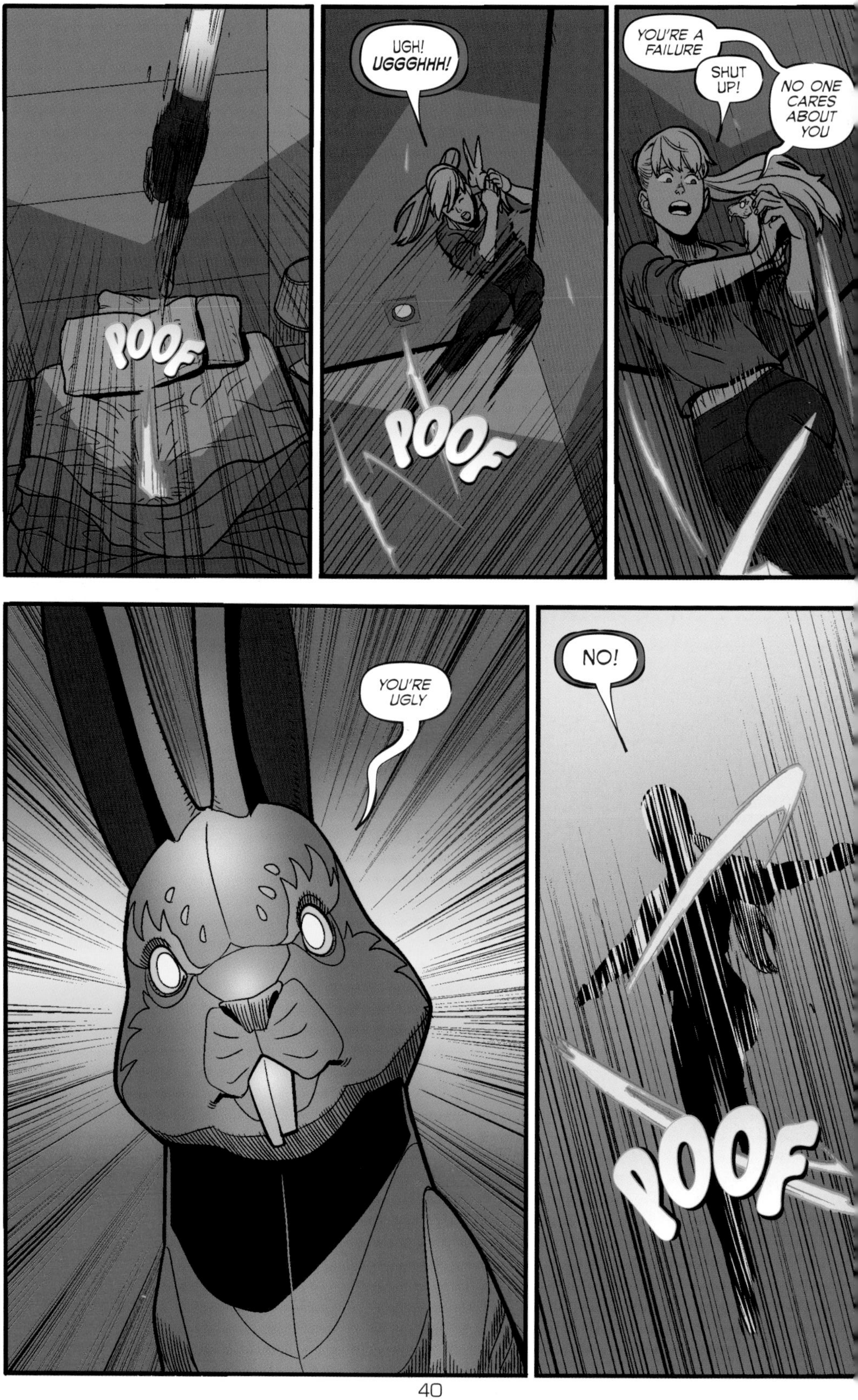
POOF
UGH! UGGGHHH!
POOF
YOU'RE A FAILURE
SHUT UP!
NO ONE CARES ABOUT YOU
YOU'RE UGLY
NO!
POOF

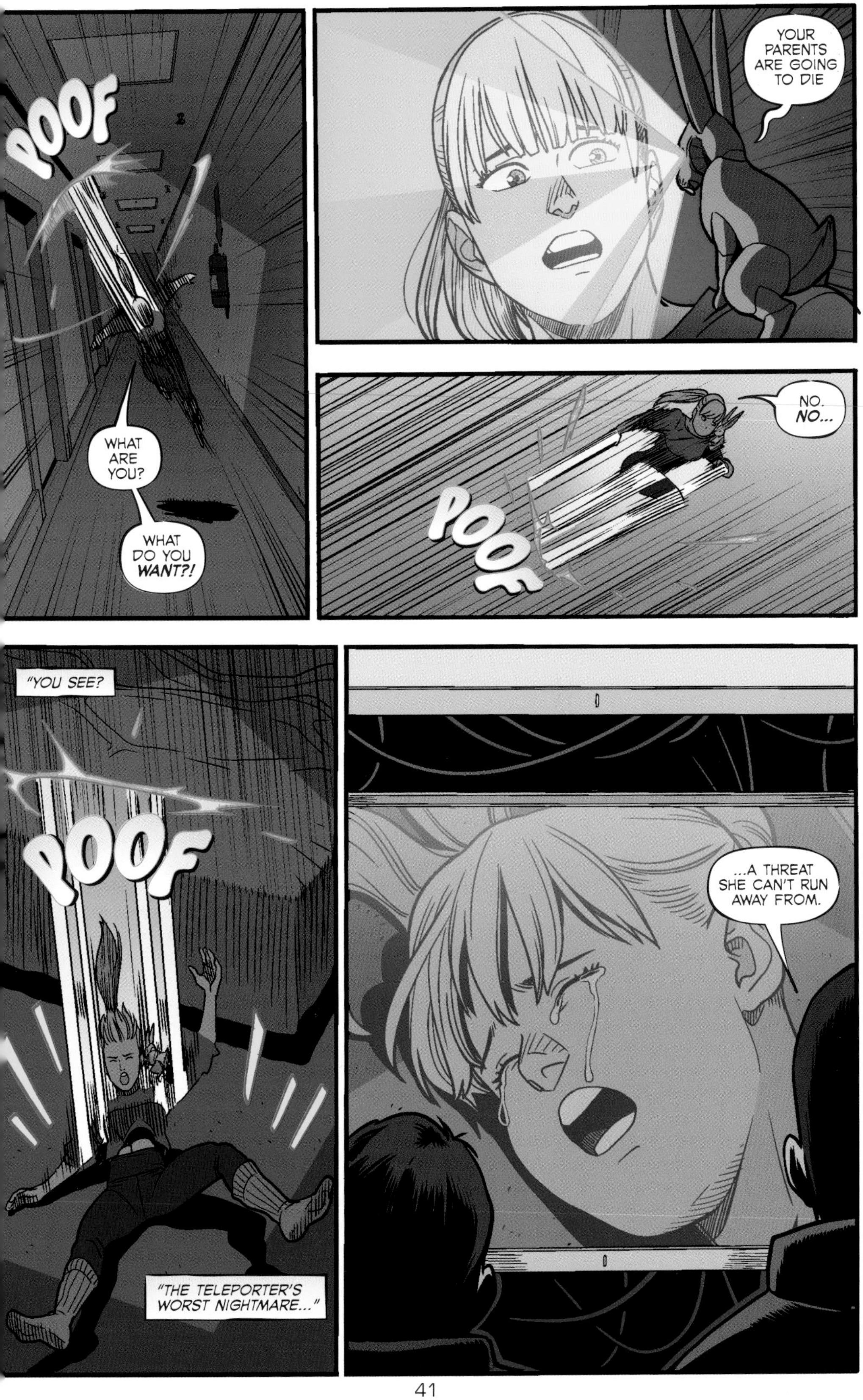
POOF
WHAT ARE YOU?
WHAT DO YOU *WANT?!*
YOUR PARENTS ARE GOING TO DIE
NO. *NO...*
POOF
"YOU SEE?
POOF
"THE TELEPORTER'S WORST NIGHTMARE..."
...A THREAT SHE CAN'T RUN AWAY FROM.

I'VE FOUGHT THAT GIRL. SHE CAN USUALLY 'PORT FARTHER THAN THAT...

THE CHI-MECHA IS INJECTING HER WITH A SEDATIVE. IT'S WEAKENING HER.

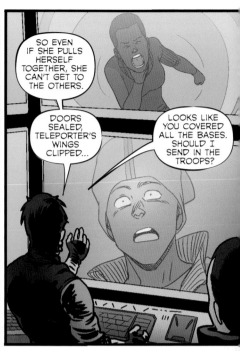

SO EVEN IF SHE PULLS HERSELF TOGETHER, SHE CAN'T GET TO THE OTHERS.

DOORS SEALED, TELEPORTER'S WINGS CLIPPED...

LOOKS LIKE YOU COVERED ALL THE BASES. SHOULD I SEND IN THE TROOPS?

PREPARE FOR THE STRIKE-- BUT WAIT FOR MY ORDER.

WE MUST GIVE THE CHI-MECHAS TIME TO FINISH THEIR WORK.

IN THE MEANTIME...

"...I WILL SAVOR THE AGONY OF MY FOES."

UGH!

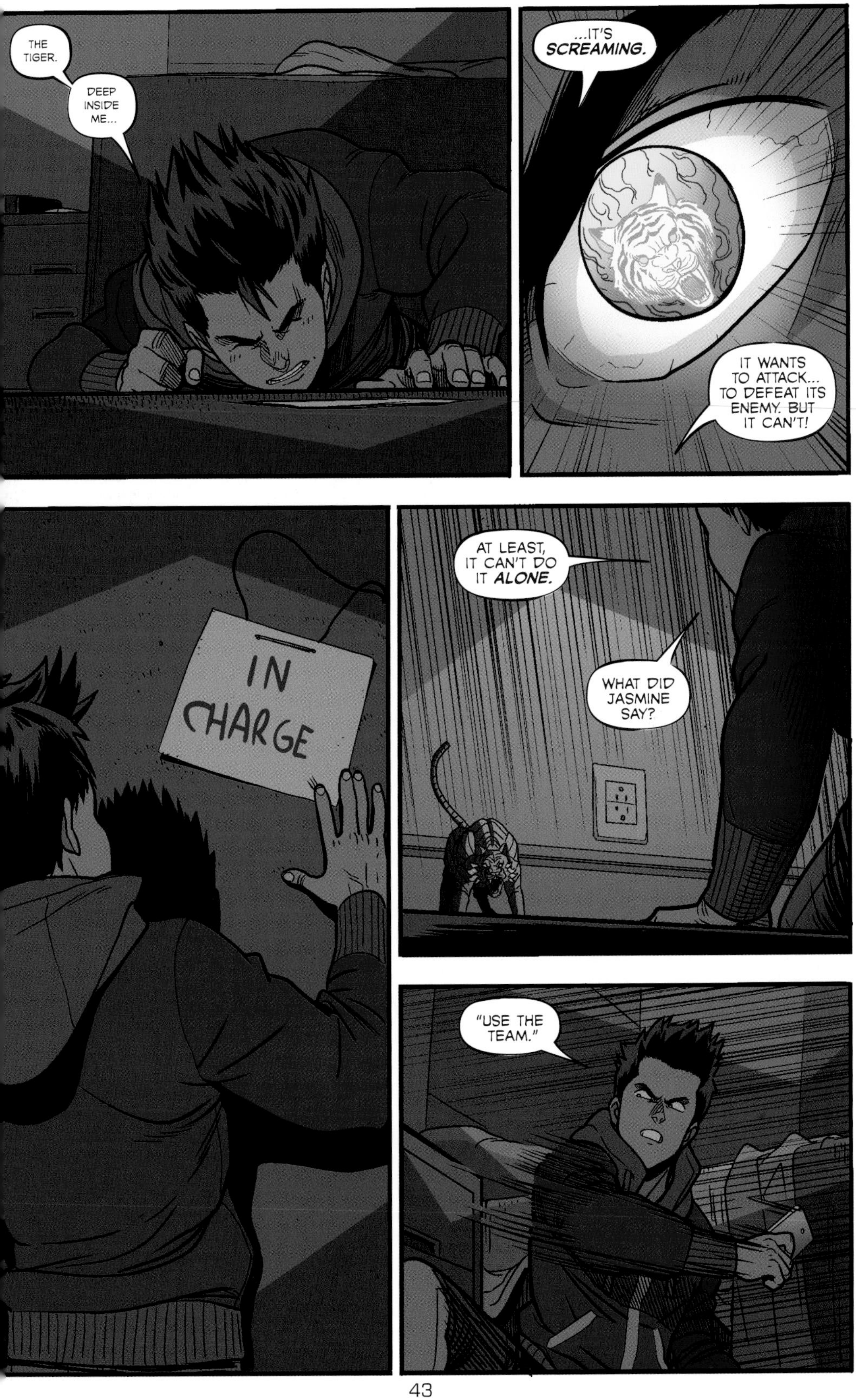
THE TIGER.
DEEP INSIDE ME...
...IT'S *SCREAMING.*
IT WANTS TO ATTACK... TO DEFEAT ITS ENEMY. BUT IT CAN'T!
IN CHARGE
AT LEAST, IT CAN'T DO IT *ALONE.*
WHAT DID JASMINE SAY?
"USE THE TEAM."

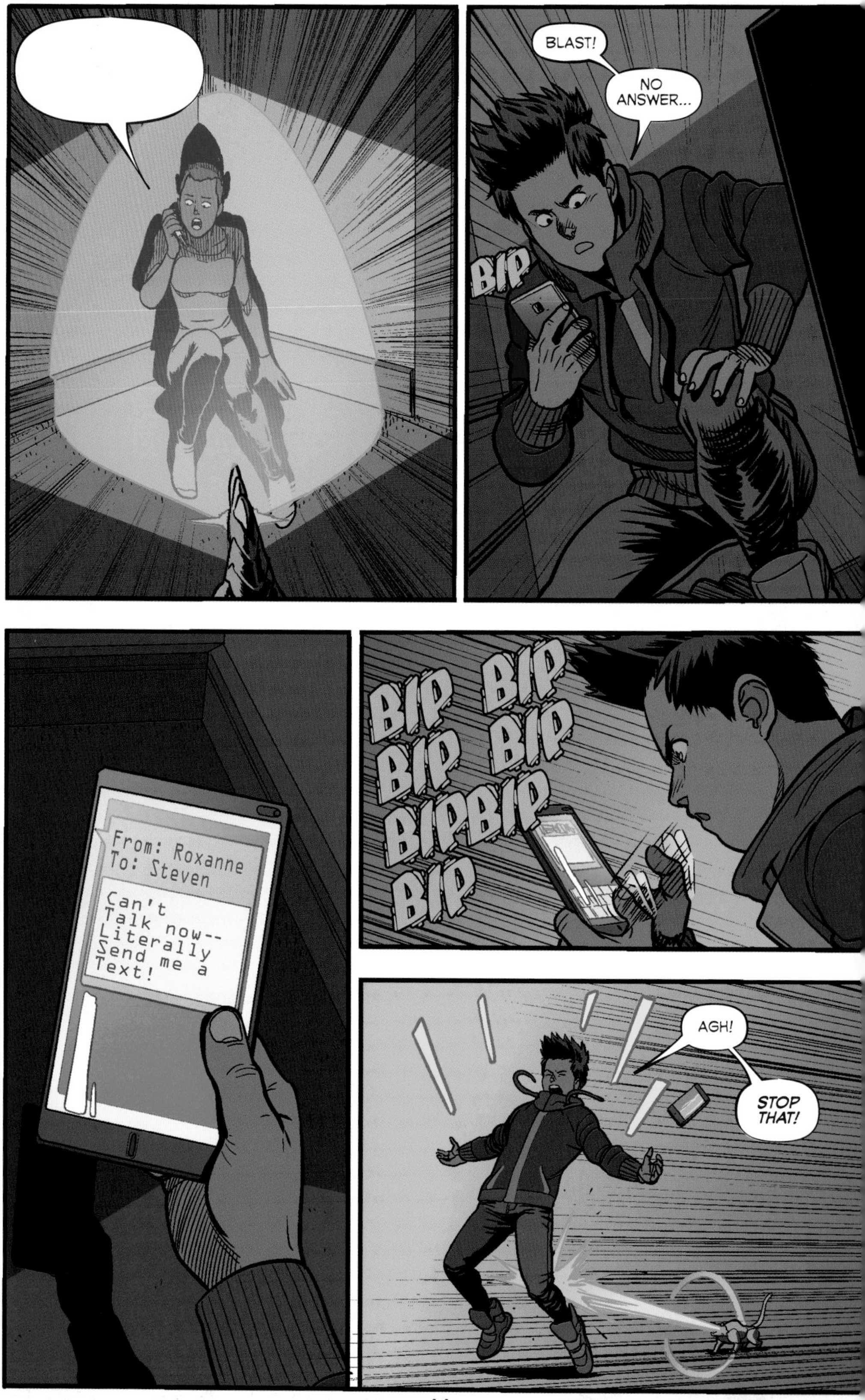
BLAST!
NO ANSWER...
BIP
From: Roxanne
To: Steven
Can't Talk now-- Literally Send me a Text!
BIP BIP
BIP BIP
BIPBIP
BIP
AGH!
STOP THAT!

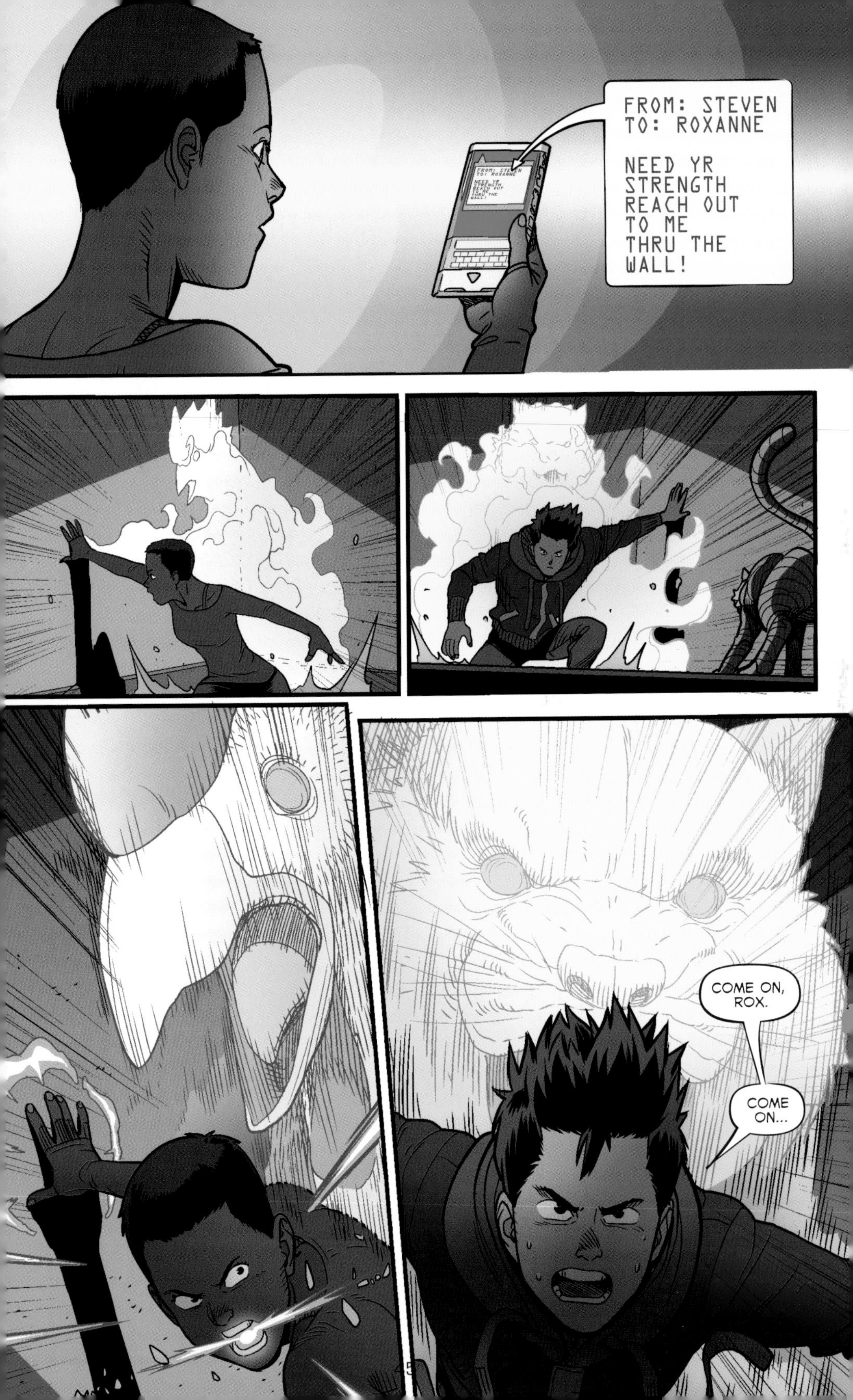
FROM: STEVEN
TO: ROXANNE
NEED YR STRENGTH REACH OUT TO ME THRU THE WALL!
COME ON, ROX.
COME ON...

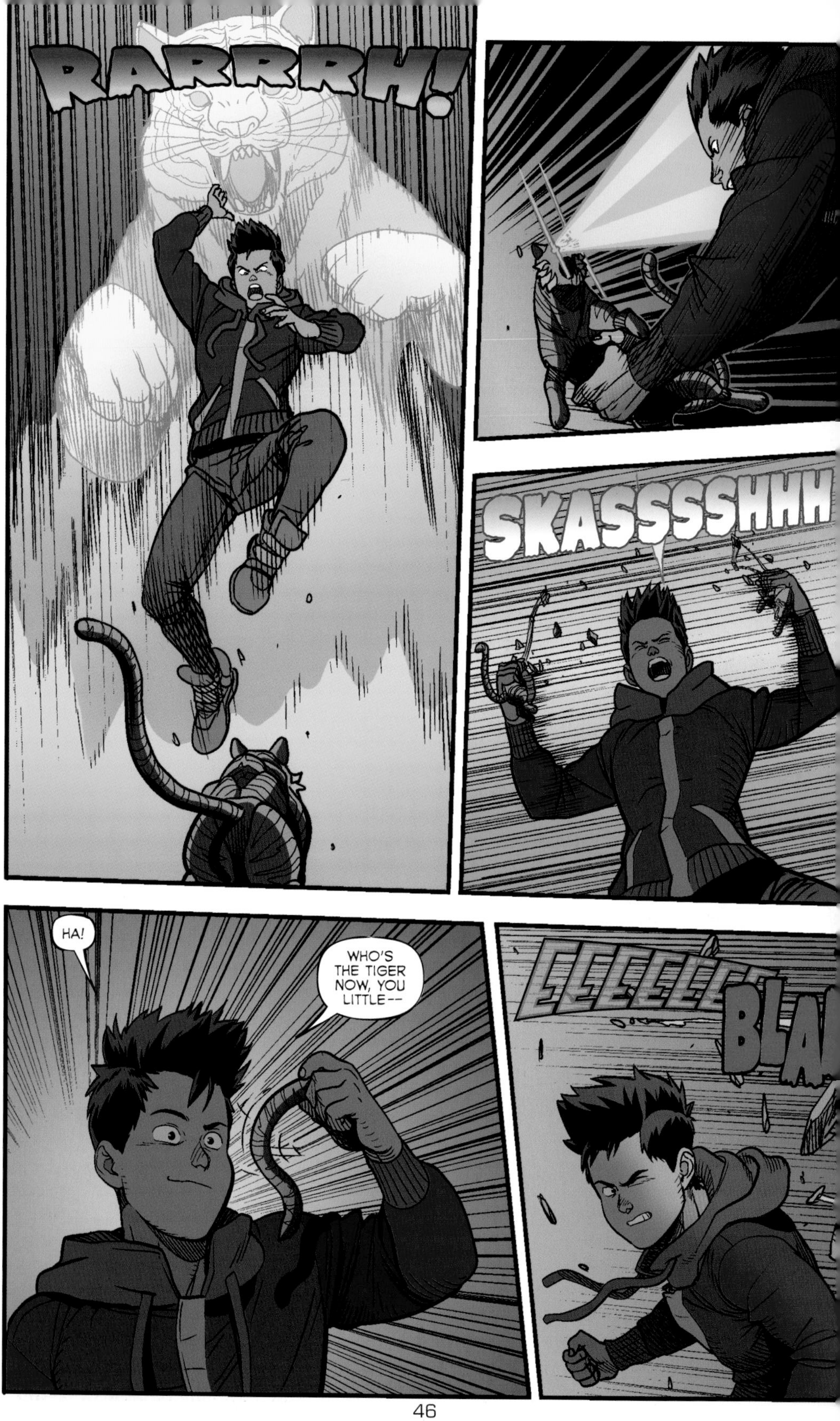
RARRRH!
SKASSSSHHH
HA!
WHO'S THE TIGER NOW, YOU LITTLE--

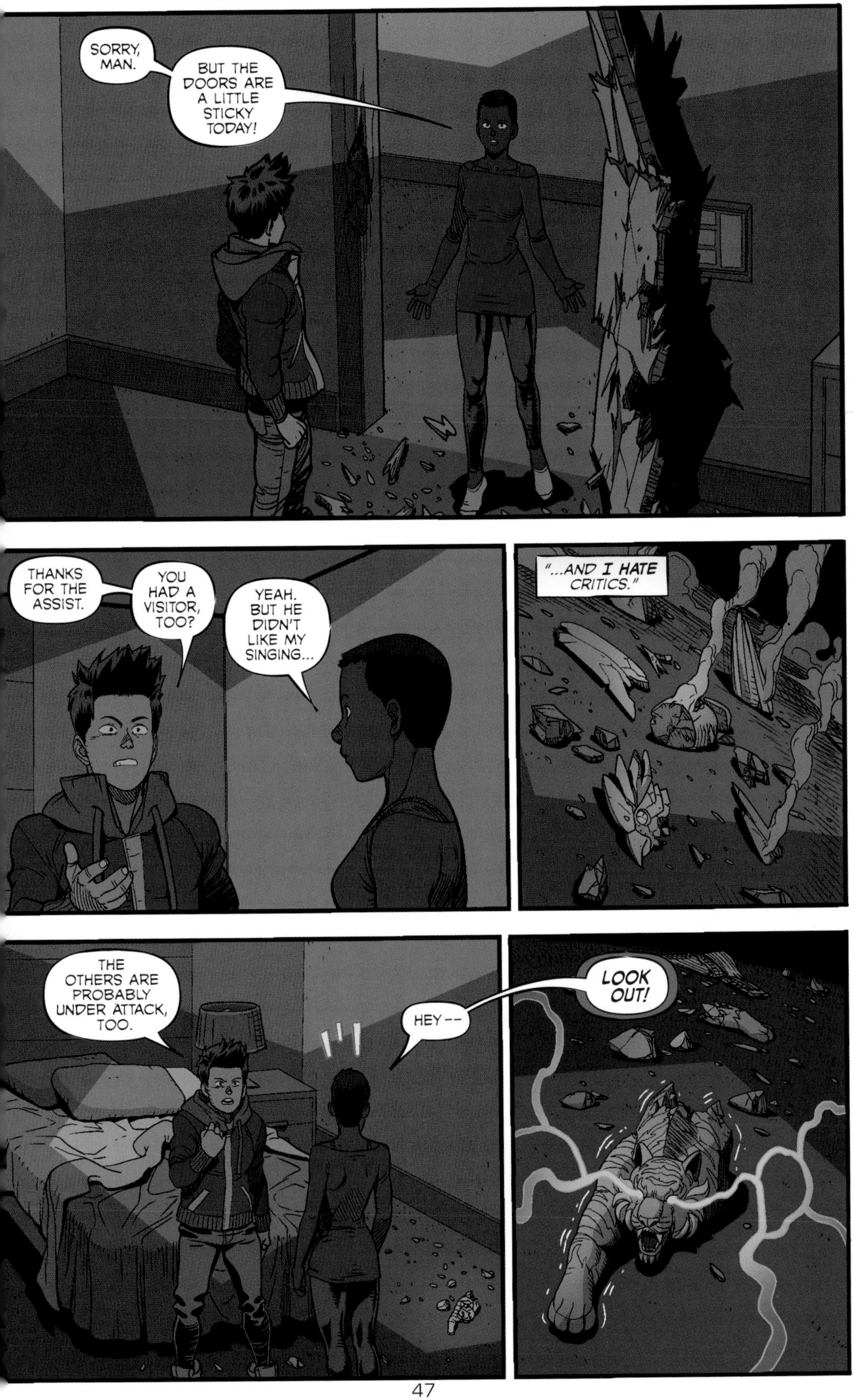
SORRY, MAN.
BUT THE DOORS ARE A LITTLE STICKY TODAY!
THANKS FOR THE ASSIST.
YOU HAD A VISITOR, TOO?
YEAH. BUT HE DIDN'T LIKE MY SINGING...
"...AND I HATE CRITICS."
THE OTHERS ARE PROBABLY UNDER ATTACK, TOO.
HEY--
LOOK OUT!

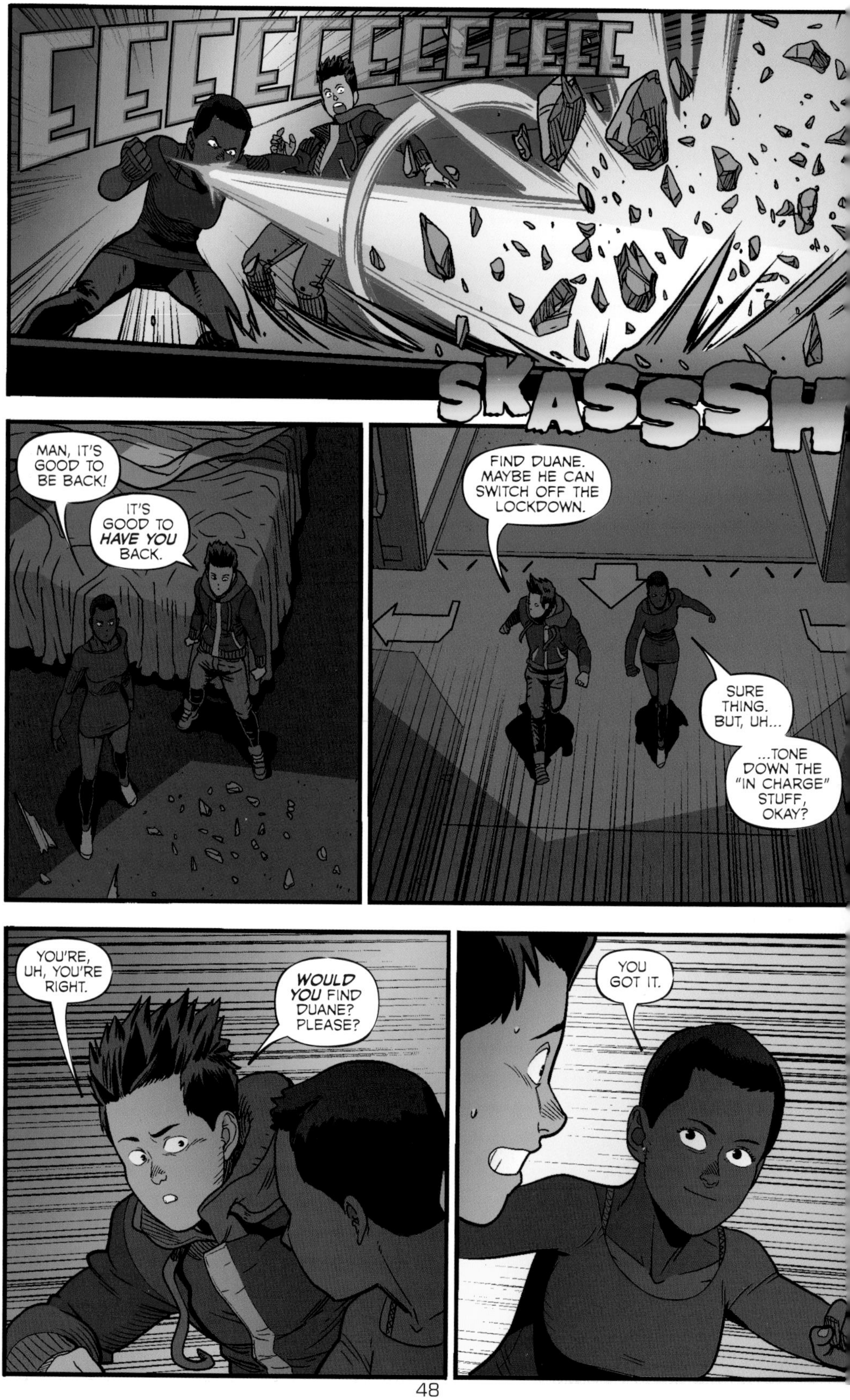

EEEEEEEEEEEE
SKASSSH
MAN, IT'S GOOD TO BE BACK!
IT'S GOOD TO **HAVE YOU** BACK.
FIND DUANE. MAYBE HE CAN SWITCH OFF THE LOCKDOWN.
SURE THING. BUT, UH...
...TONE DOWN THE "IN CHARGE" STUFF, OKAY?
YOU'RE, UH, YOU'RE RIGHT.
WOULD YOU FIND DUANE? PLEASE?
YOU GOT IT.

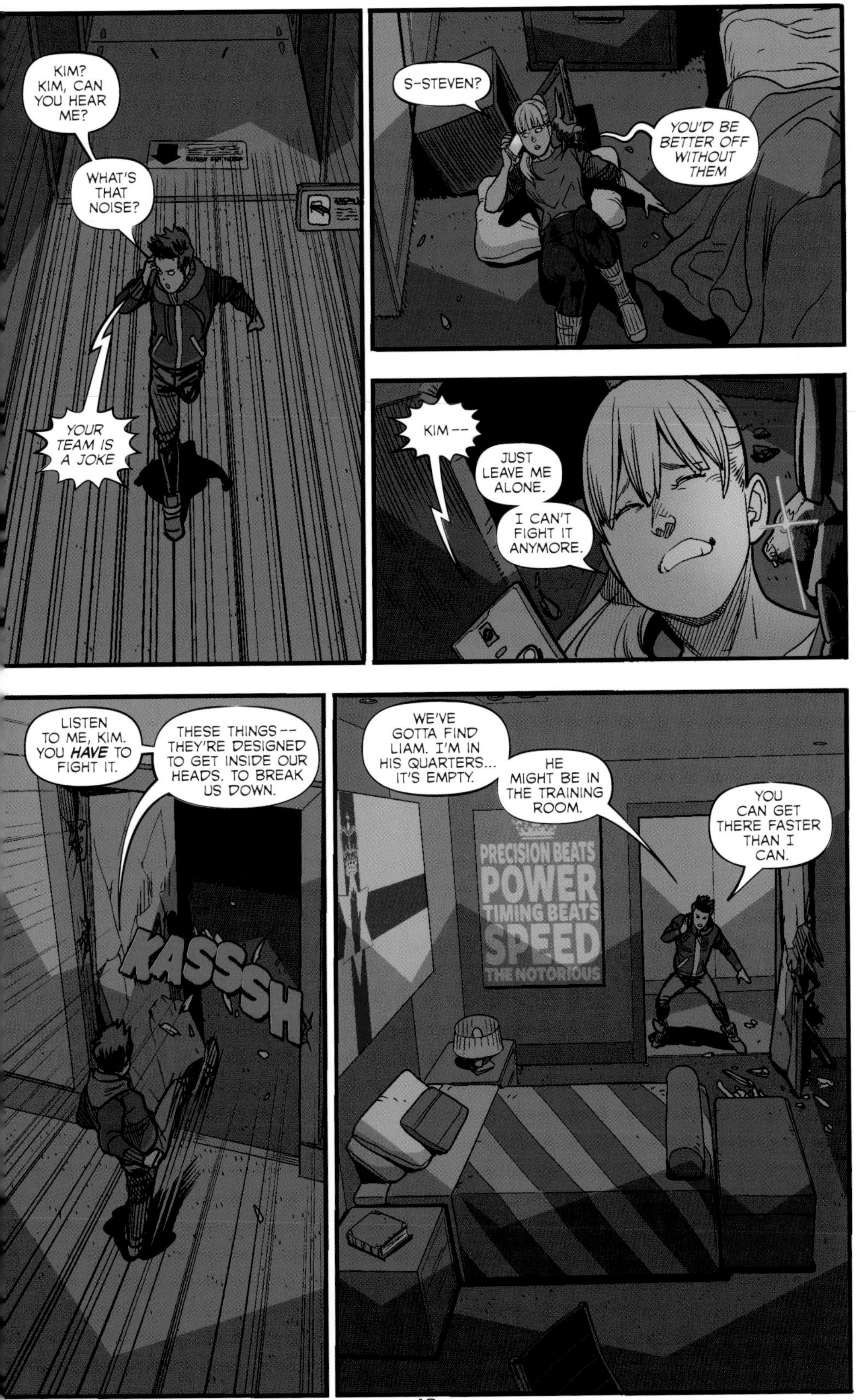

KIM? KIM, CAN YOU HEAR ME?
WHAT'S THAT NOISE?
YOUR TEAM IS A JOKE
S-STEVEN?
YOU'D BE BETTER OFF WITHOUT THEM
KIM--
JUST LEAVE ME ALONE.
I CAN'T FIGHT IT ANYMORE.
LISTEN TO ME, KIM. YOU ***HAVE*** TO FIGHT IT.
THESE THINGS-- THEY'RE DESIGNED TO GET INSIDE OUR HEADS. TO BREAK US DOWN.
KASSSH
WE'VE GOTTA FIND LIAM. I'M IN HIS QUARTERS... IT'S EMPTY.
HE MIGHT BE IN THE TRAINING ROOM.
YOU CAN GET THERE FASTER THAN I CAN.
PRECISION BEATS POWER TIMING BEATS SPEED THE NOTORIOUS

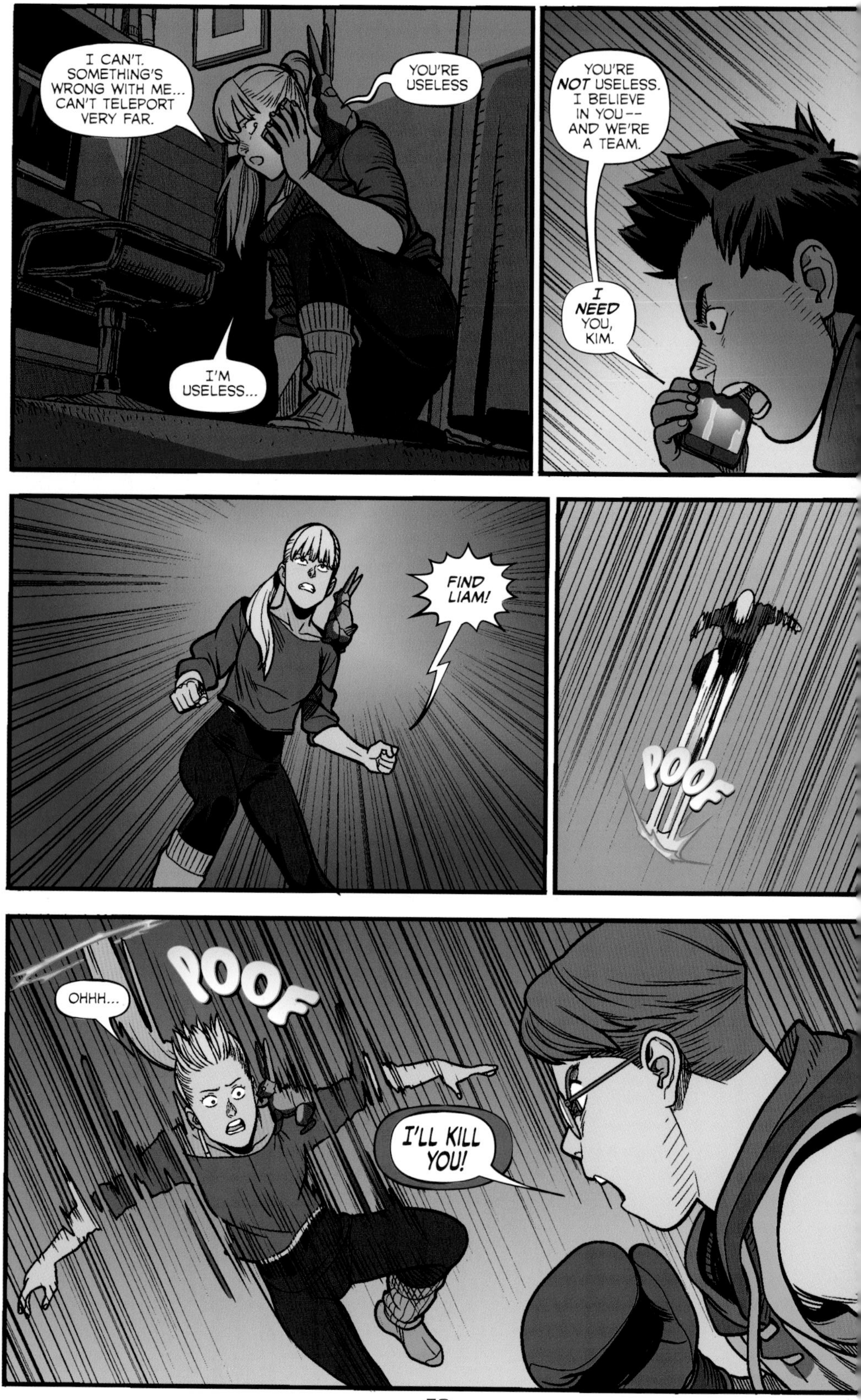
I CAN'T. SOMETHING'S WRONG WITH ME... CAN'T TELEPORT VERY FAR.
YOU'RE USELESS
I'M USELESS...
YOU'RE NOT USELESS. I BELIEVE IN YOU-- AND WE'RE A TEAM.
I NEED YOU, KIM.
FIND LIAM!
POOF
POOF
OHHH...
I'LL KILL YOU!

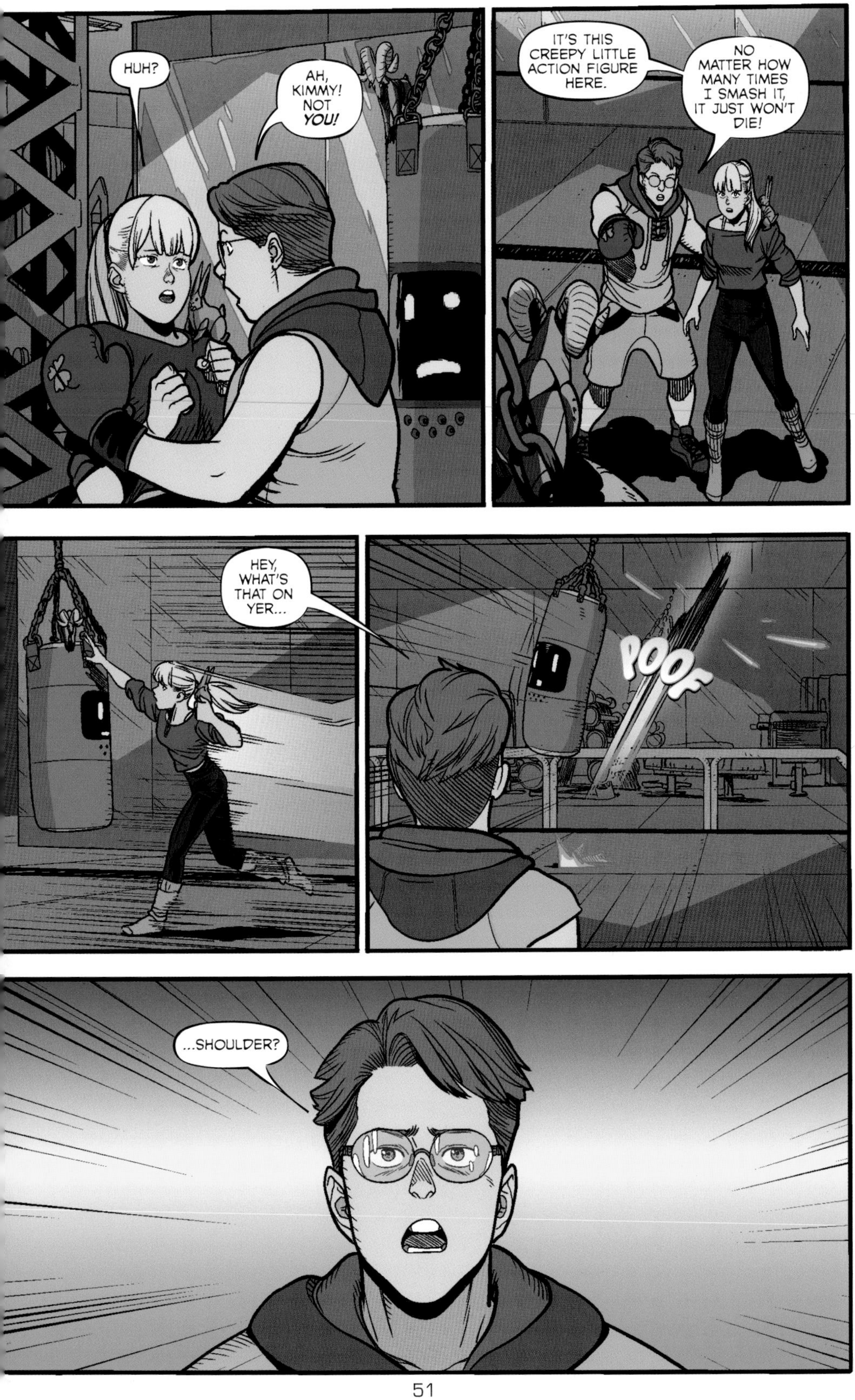
HUH?
AH, KIMMY! NOT YOU!
IT'S THIS CREEPY LITTLE ACTION FIGURE HERE.
NO MATTER HOW MANY TIMES I SMASH IT, IT JUST WON'T DIE!
HEY, WHAT'S THAT ON YER...
POOF
...SHOULDER?

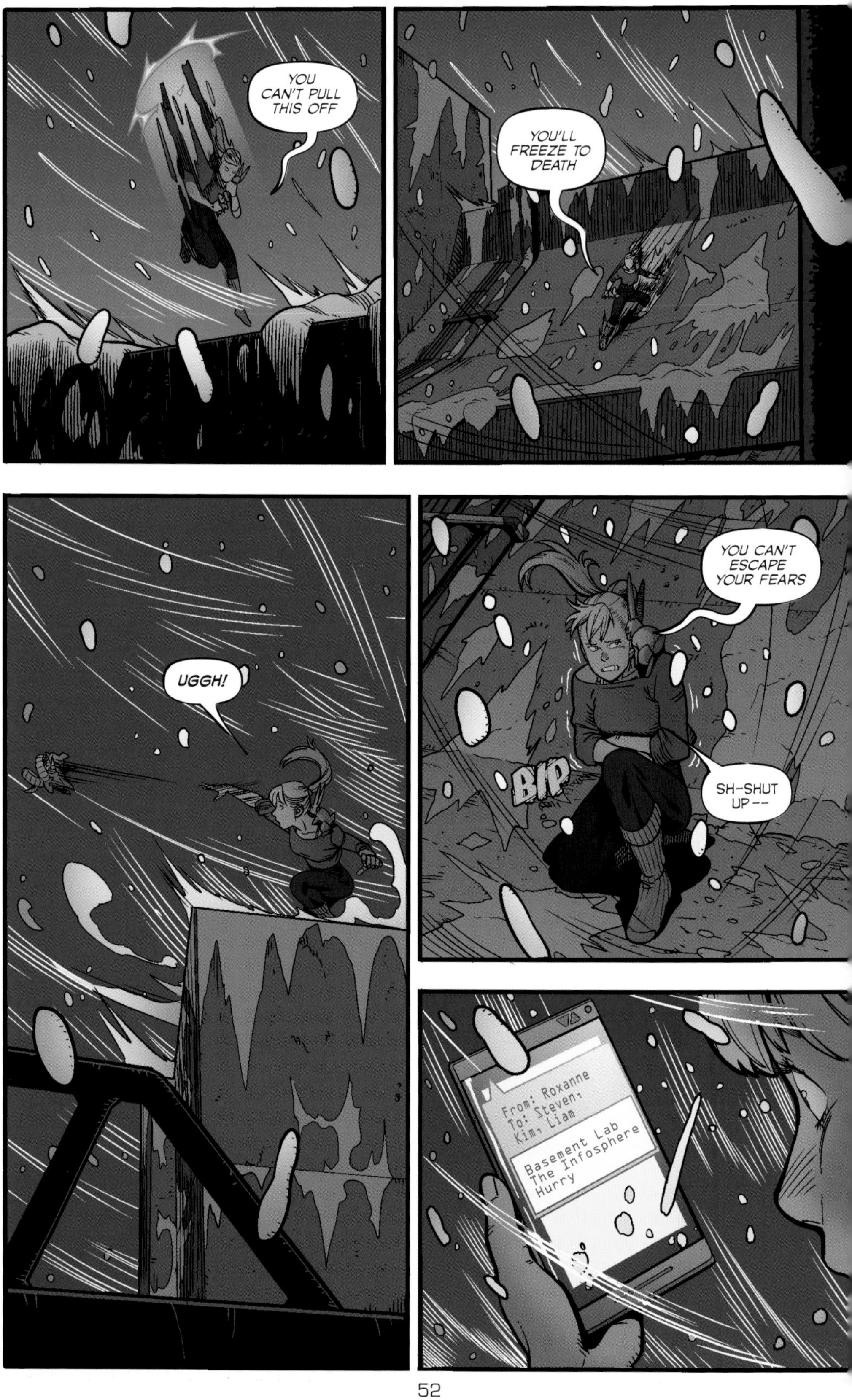
YOU CAN'T PULL THIS OFF
YOU'LL FREEZE TO DEATH
UGGH!
YOU CAN'T ESCAPE YOUR FEARS
BIP
SH-SHUT UP--
From: Roxanne
To: Steven, Kim, Liam
Basement Lab
The Infosphere
Hurry

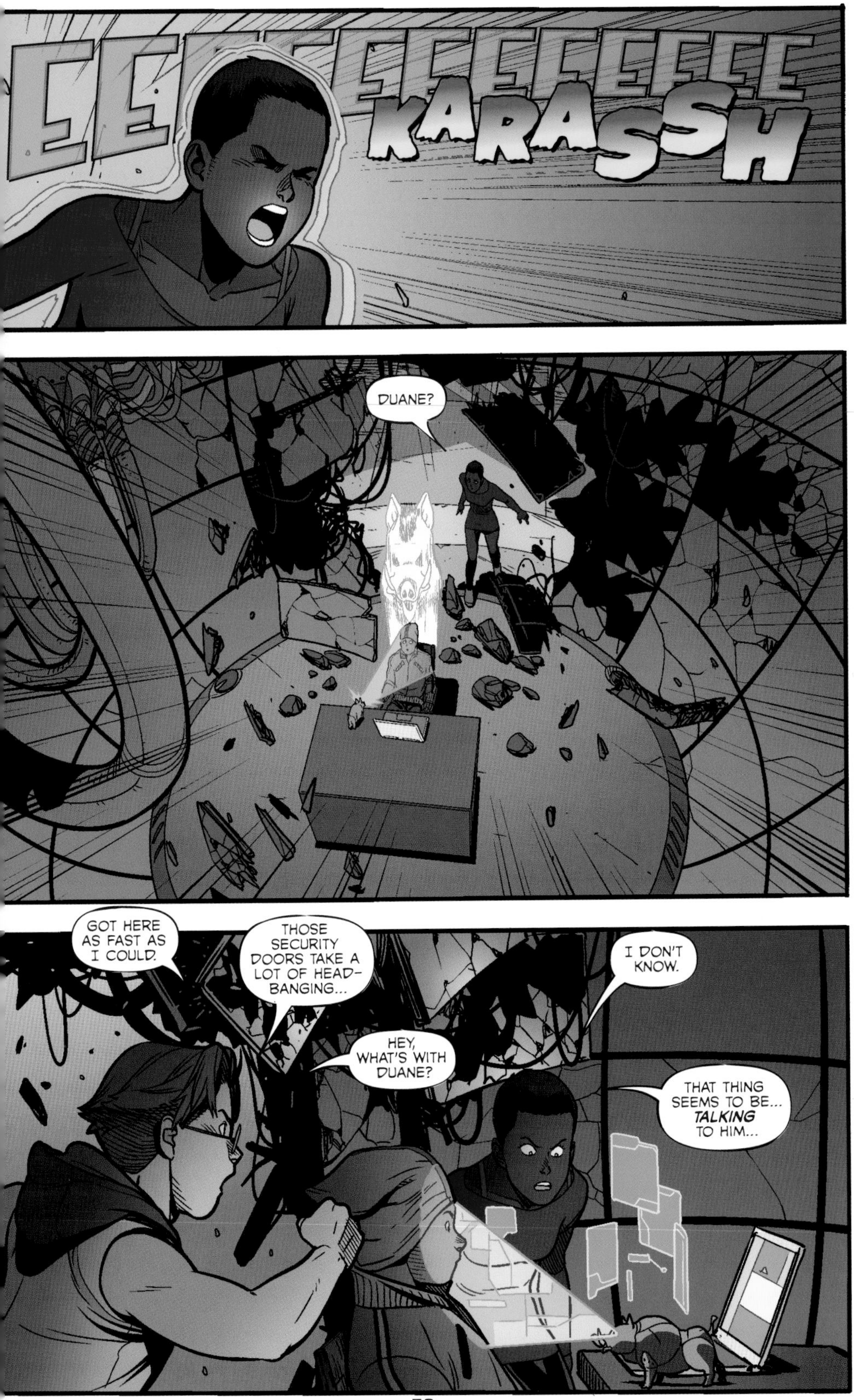
EEEEEEEEEEEE
KARASSH
DUANE?
GOT HERE AS FAST AS I COULD.
THOSE SECURITY DOORS TAKE A LOT OF HEAD-BANGING...
HEY, WHAT'S WITH DUANE?
I DON'T KNOW.
THAT THING SEEMS TO BE... *TALKING* TO HIM...

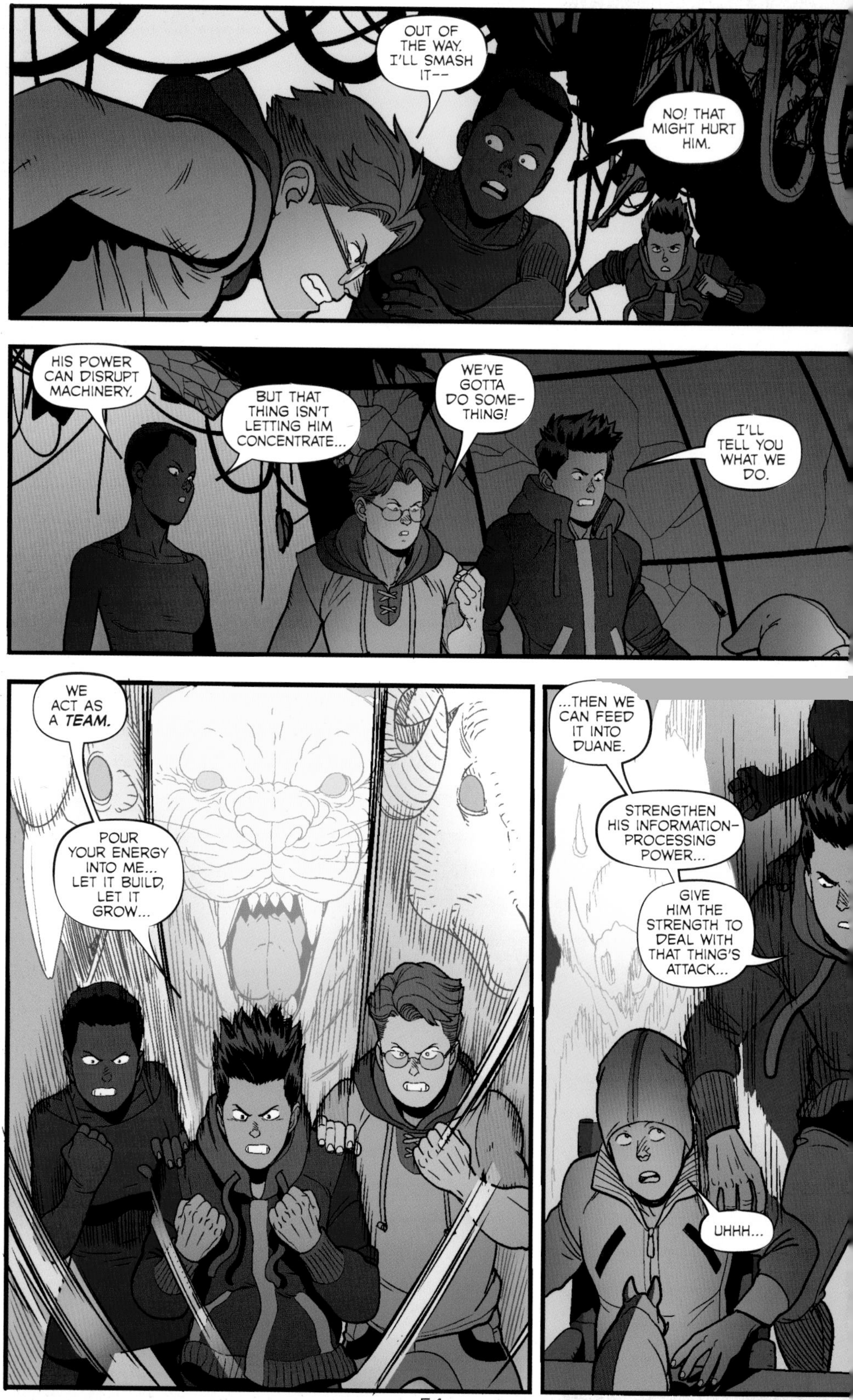
OUT OF THE WAY. I'LL SMASH IT--
NO! THAT MIGHT HURT HIM.
HIS POWER CAN DISRUPT MACHINERY.
BUT THAT THING ISN'T LETTING HIM CONCENTRATE...
WE'VE GOTTA DO SOME-THING!
I'LL TELL YOU WHAT WE DO.
WE ACT AS A *TEAM.*
POUR YOUR ENERGY INTO ME... LET IT BUILD, LET IT GROW...
...THEN WE CAN FEED IT INTO DUANE.
STRENGTHEN HIS INFORMATION-PROCESSING POWER...
GIVE HIM THE STRENGTH TO DEAL WITH THAT THING'S ATTACK...
UHHH...

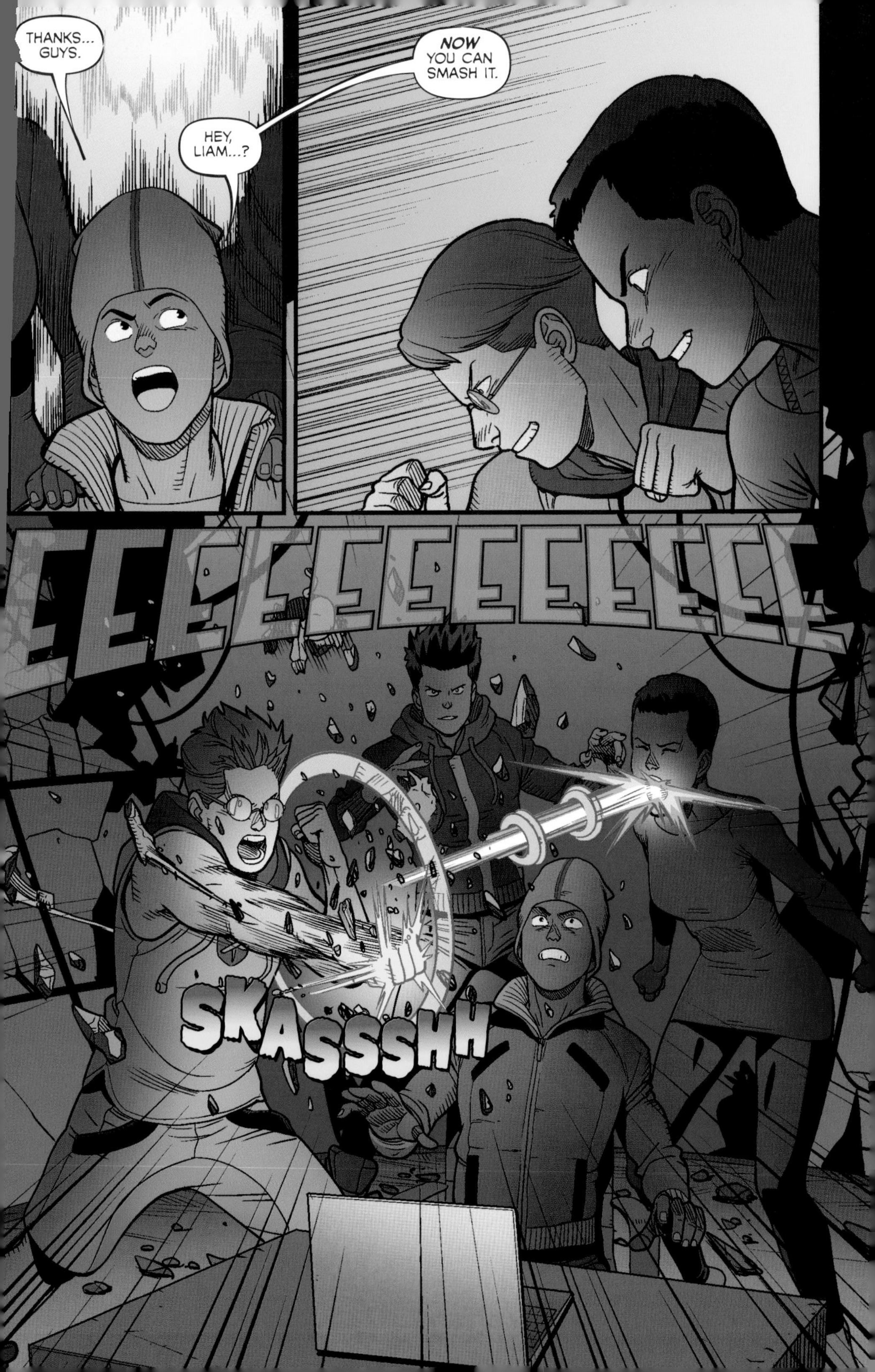
THANKS... GUYS.
HEY, LIAM...?
NOW YOU CAN SMASH IT.
EEEEEEEEEEEEE
SKASSSHH

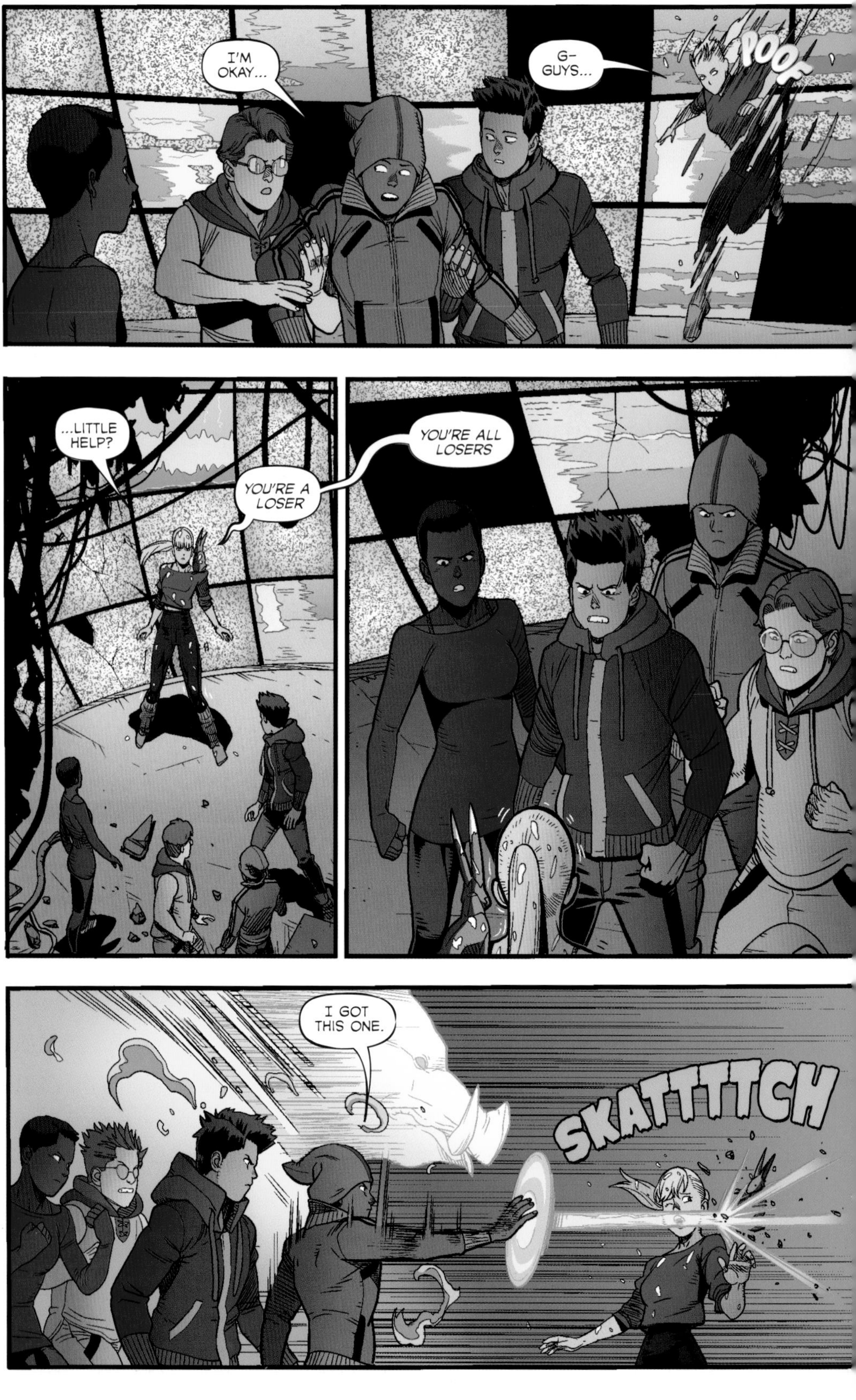
I'M OKAY...
G– GUYS...
POOF
...LITTLE HELP?
YOU'RE A LOSER
YOU'RE ALL LOSERS
I GOT THIS ONE.
SKATTTTCH

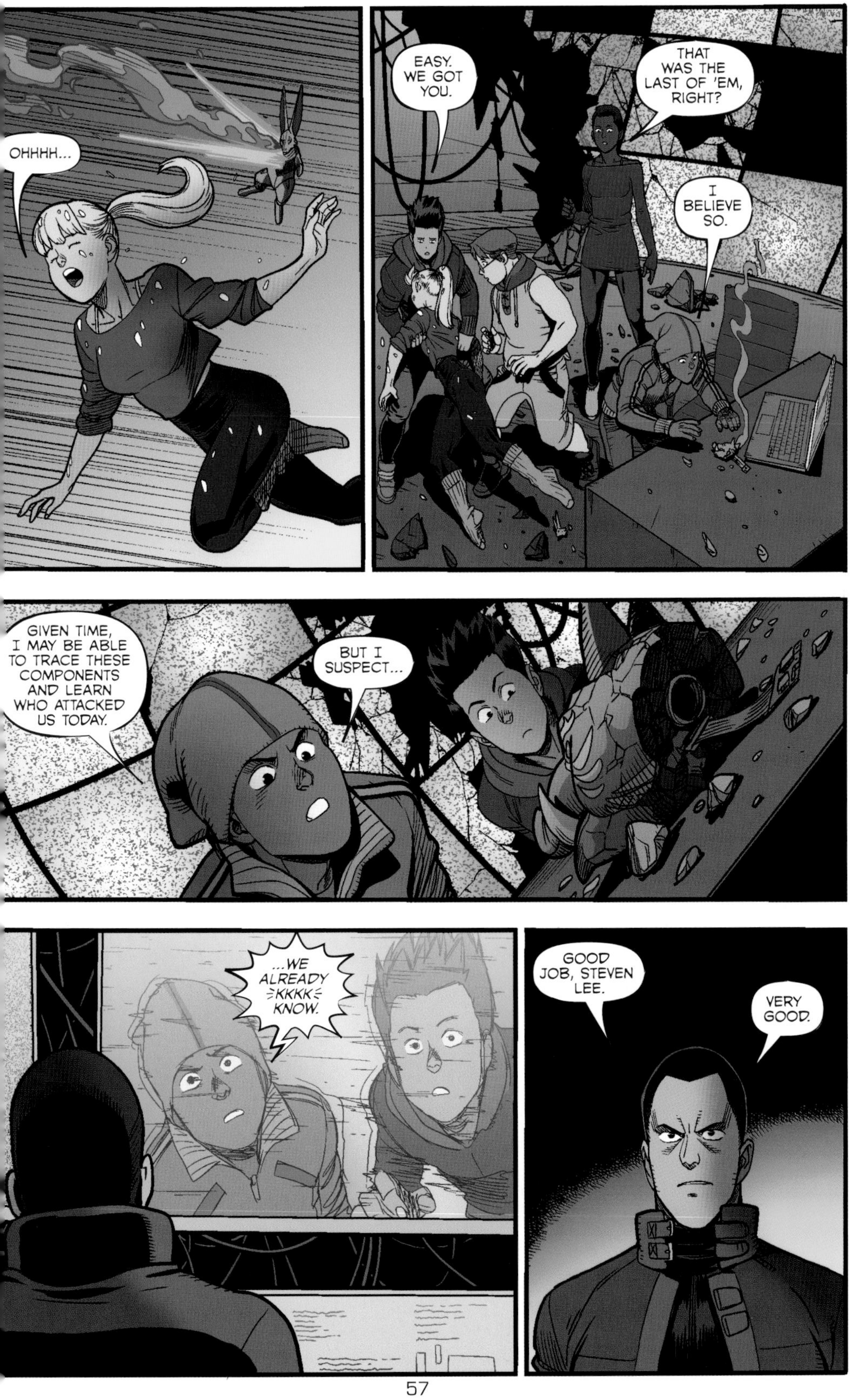
OHHHH...
EASY. WE GOT YOU.
THAT WAS THE LAST OF 'EM, RIGHT?
I BELIEVE SO.
GIVEN TIME, I MAY BE ABLE TO TRACE THESE COMPONENTS AND LEARN WHO ATTACKED US TODAY.
BUT I SUSPECT...
...WE ALREADY =KKKK= KNOW.
GOOD JOB, STEVEN LEE.
VERY GOOD.

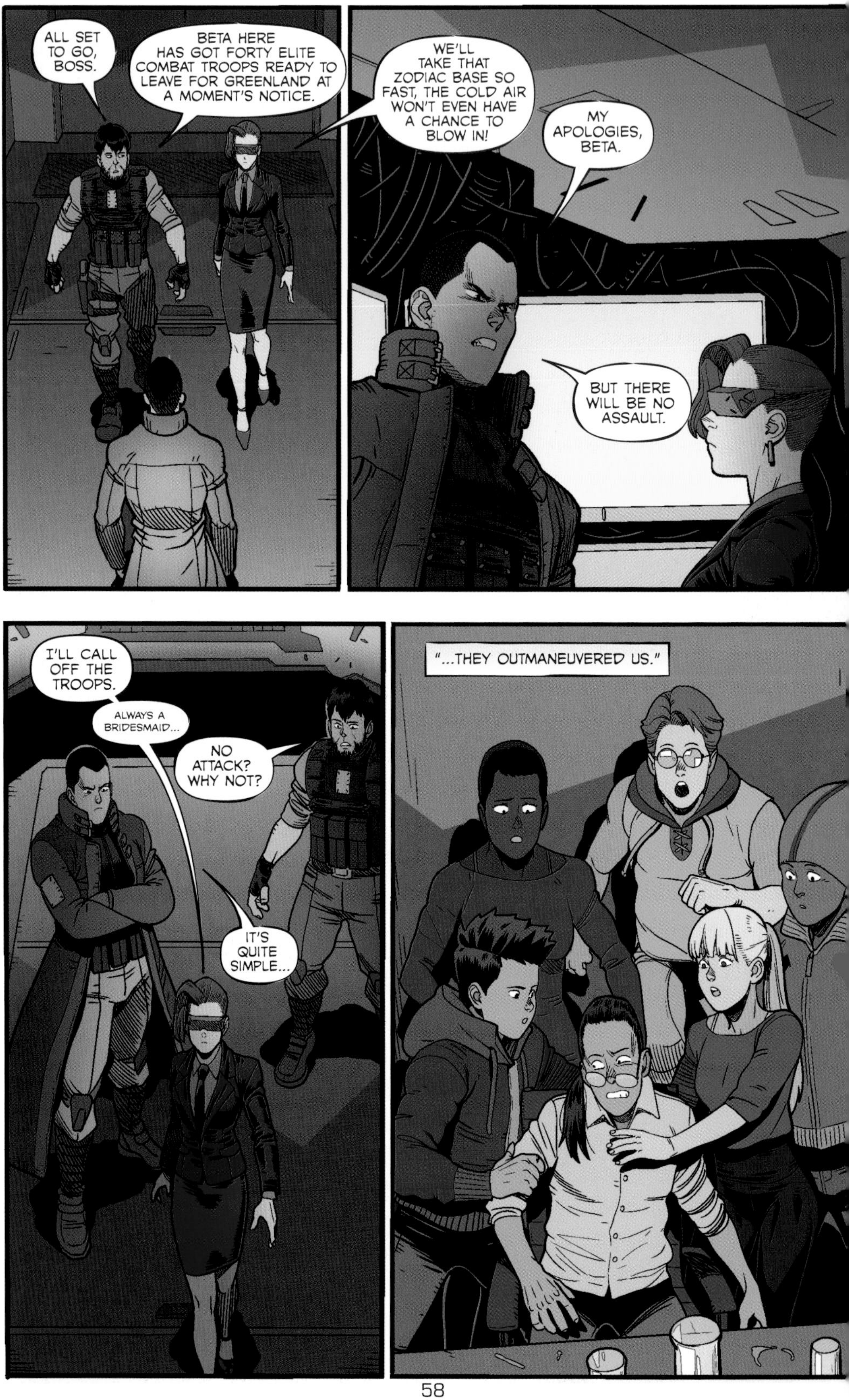
ALL SET TO GO, BOSS.
BETA HERE HAS GOT FORTY ELITE COMBAT TROOPS READY TO LEAVE FOR GREENLAND AT A MOMENT'S NOTICE.
WE'LL TAKE THAT ZODIAC BASE SO FAST, THE COLD AIR WON'T EVEN HAVE A CHANCE TO BLOW IN!
MY APOLOGIES, BETA.
BUT THERE WILL BE NO ASSAULT.
I'LL CALL OFF THE TROOPS.
ALWAYS A BRIDESMAID...
NO ATTACK? WHY NOT?
IT'S QUITE SIMPLE...
"...THEY OUTMANEUVERED US."

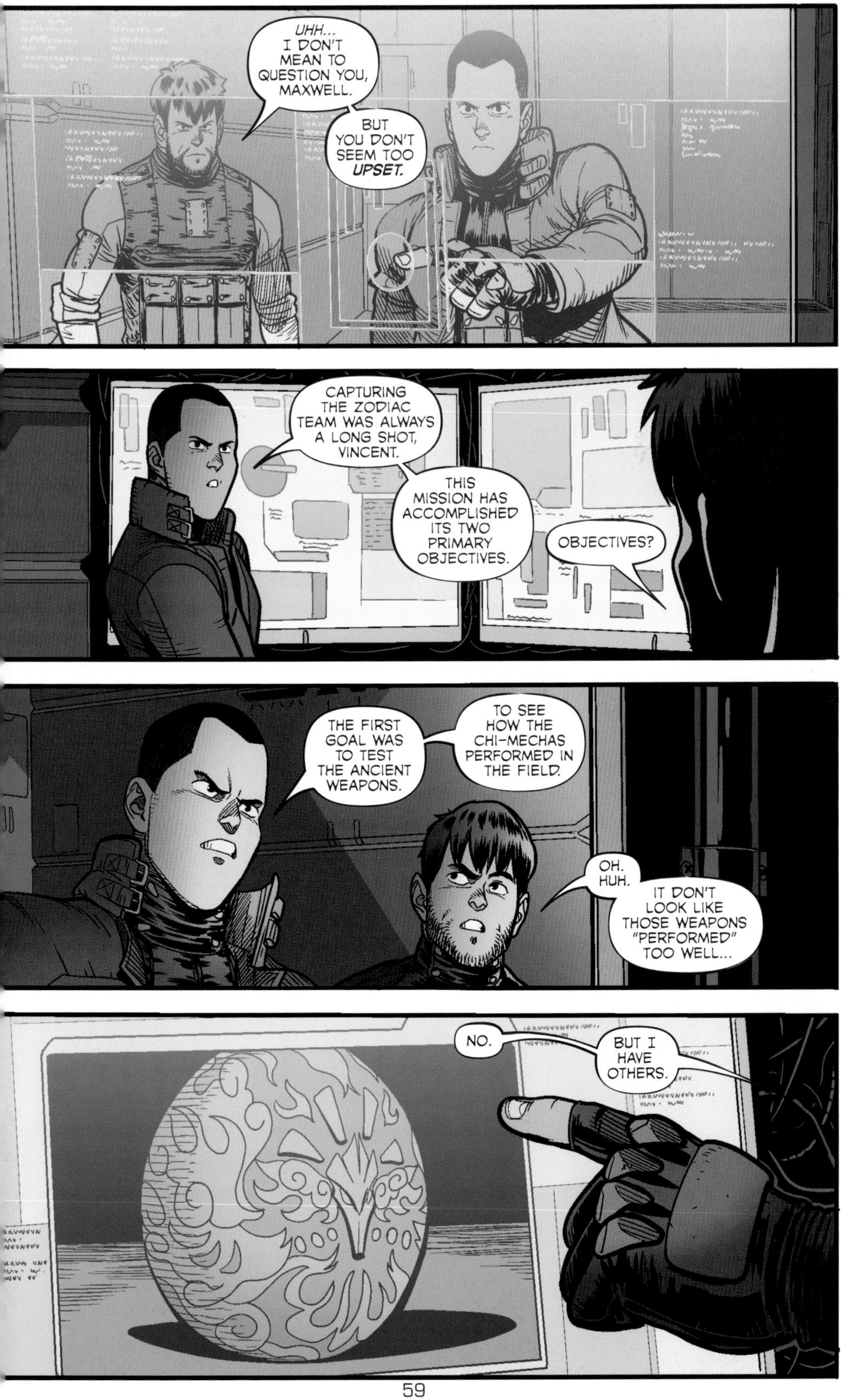

UHH... I DON'T MEAN TO QUESTION YOU, MAXWELL.
BUT YOU DON'T SEEM TOO *UPSET.*
CAPTURING THE ZODIAC TEAM WAS ALWAYS A LONG SHOT, VINCENT.
THIS MISSION HAS ACCOMPLISHED ITS TWO PRIMARY OBJECTIVES.
OBJECTIVES?
THE FIRST GOAL WAS TO TEST THE ANCIENT WEAPONS.
TO SEE HOW THE CHI-MECHAS PERFORMED IN THE FIELD.
OH. HUH.
IT DON'T LOOK LIKE THOSE WEAPONS "PERFORMED" TOO WELL...
NO.
BUT I HAVE OTHERS.

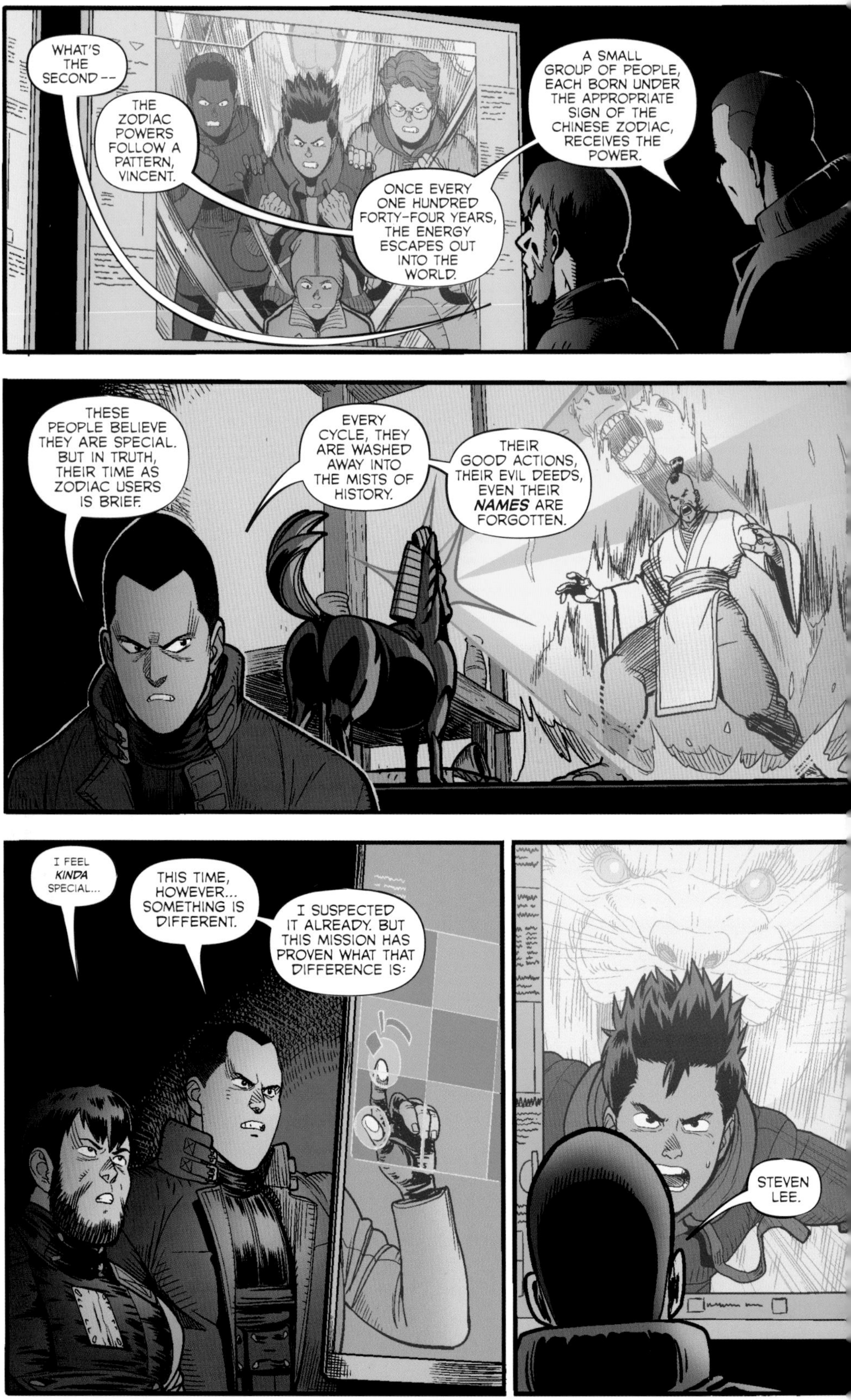

WHAT'S THE SECOND --
THE ZODIAC POWERS FOLLOW A PATTERN, VINCENT.
ONCE EVERY ONE HUNDRED FORTY-FOUR YEARS, THE ENERGY ESCAPES OUT INTO THE WORLD.
A SMALL GROUP OF PEOPLE, EACH BORN UNDER THE APPROPRIATE SIGN OF THE CHINESE ZODIAC, RECEIVES THE POWER.
THESE PEOPLE BELIEVE THEY ARE SPECIAL. BUT IN TRUTH, THEIR TIME AS ZODIAC USERS IS BRIEF.
EVERY CYCLE, THEY ARE WASHED AWAY INTO THE MISTS OF HISTORY.
THEIR GOOD ACTIONS, THEIR EVIL DEEDS, EVEN THEIR NAMES ARE FORGOTTEN.
I FEEL KINDA SPECIAL...
THIS TIME, HOWEVER... SOMETHING IS DIFFERENT.
I SUSPECTED IT ALREADY. BUT THIS MISSION HAS PROVEN WHAT THAT DIFFERENCE IS:
STEVEN LEE.

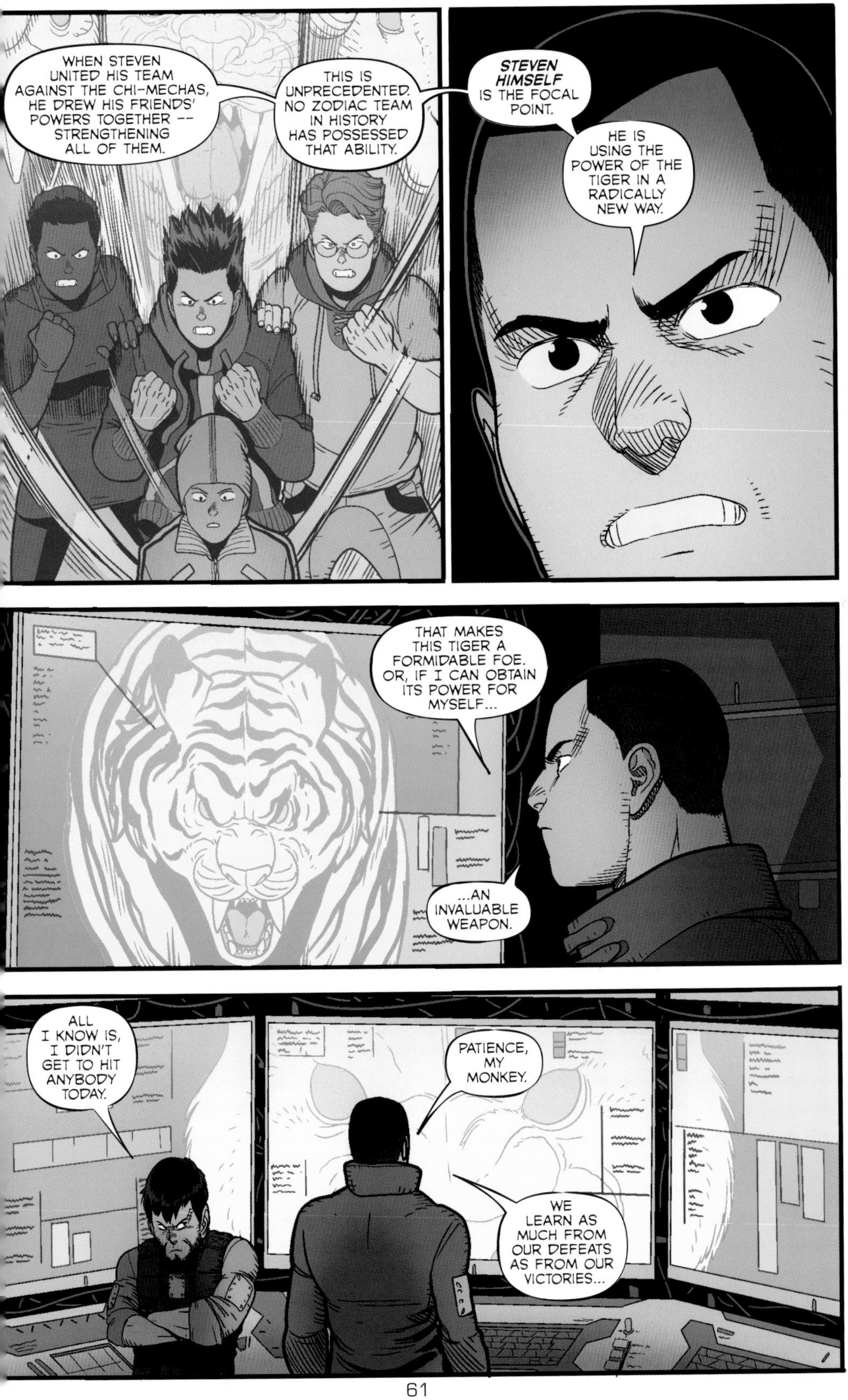
WHEN STEVEN UNITED HIS TEAM AGAINST THE CHI-MECHAS, HE DREW HIS FRIENDS' POWERS TOGETHER -- STRENGTHENING ALL OF THEM.
THIS IS UNPRECEDENTED. NO ZODIAC TEAM IN HISTORY HAS POSSESSED THAT ABILITY.
STEVEN HIMSELF IS THE FOCAL POINT.
HE IS USING THE POWER OF THE TIGER IN A RADICALLY NEW WAY.
THAT MAKES THIS TIGER A FORMIDABLE FOE. OR, IF I CAN OBTAIN ITS POWER FOR MYSELF...
...AN INVALUABLE WEAPON.
ALL I KNOW IS, I DIDN'T GET TO HIT ANYBODY TODAY.
PATIENCE, MY MONKEY.
WE LEARN AS MUCH FROM OUR DEFEATS AS FROM OUR VICTORIES...

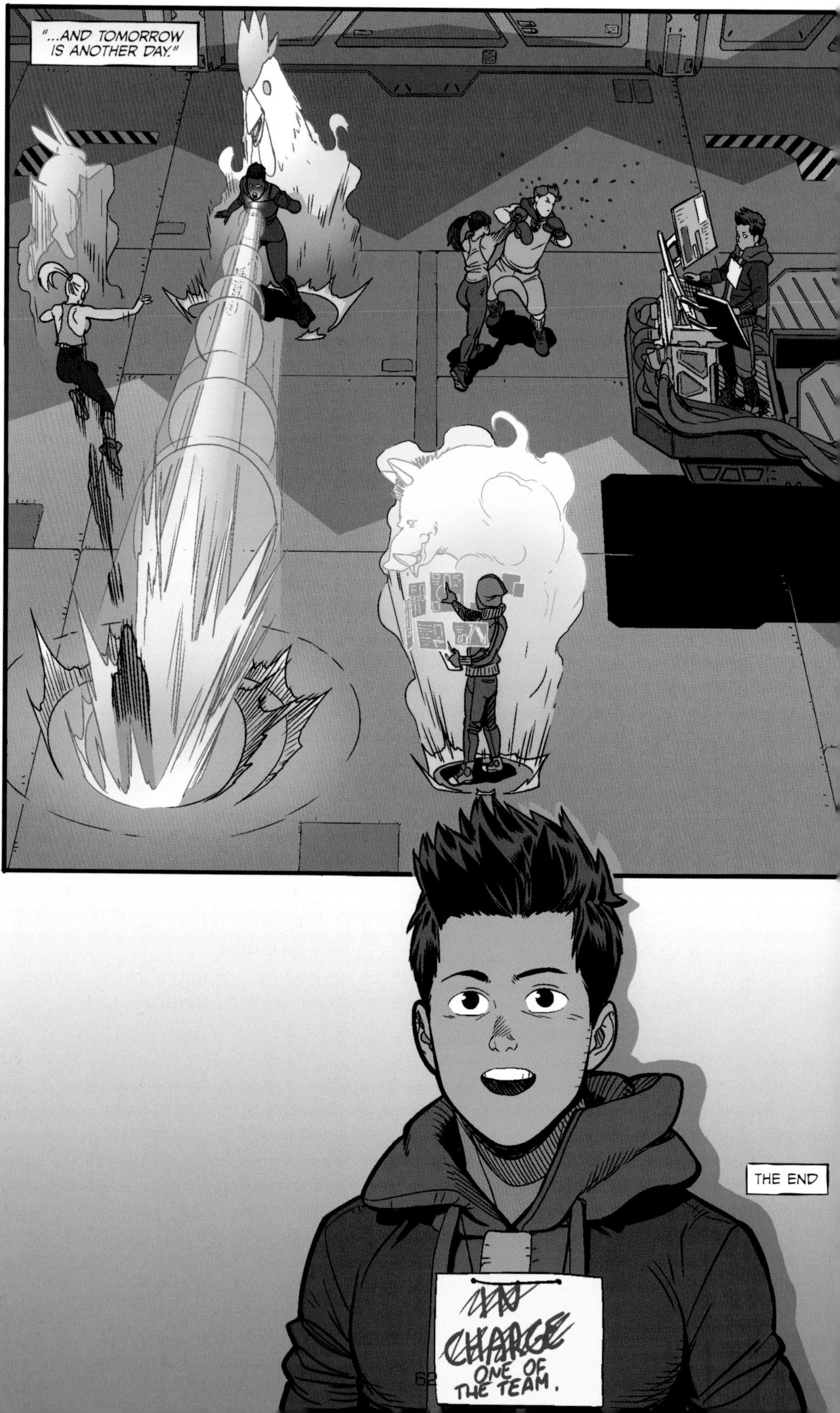
"...AND TOMORROW IS ANOTHER DAY."
THE END
CHARGE
ONE OF THE TEAM.

WATCH OUT FOR PAPERCUT**Z**

Jim Salicrup and Stan Lee together again!

Welcome to the take-no-prisoners third THE ZODIAC LEGACY graphic novel, based on the series created by Stan Lee, written by Stuart Moore, and illustrated by P.H. Marcondes, from Papercutz—that over-achieving organization dedicated to publishing great graphic novels for all ages. I'm Jim Salicrup, Editor-in-Chief and Ancient Artifact, here to talk about the creator of THE ZODIAC LEGACY, the one and only Stan Lee...

While I was just joking about being an "Ancient Artifact," it does amuse me that Steven Lee is 15-years old, the same age I was back in 1972 when I first started working for my hero Stan Lee. But now that I'm editing, along with Assistant Managing Editor Jeff Whitman, THE ZODIAC LEGACY, I'm now older than Stan Lee was when I first started working for him. If you're good at math puzzles, all you need to know is that Stan Lee is now 94-years old to figure out how old he was back then and how old I am now. For a further hint, I can reveal that I was born in the Year of the Rooster, while Stan was born in the Year of the Dog.

It all started when I made the generous offer to be a slave for Marvel Comics, in response I was invited down to their Madison Avenue headquarters. Let's just think about that for a second or three... Can you imagine what the odds are today of someone even getting a response—let alone an actual invitation to visit the legendary Marvel Bullpen? All in response to a silly offer from a fifteen year-old fan from The Bronx? In so many ways this was like I just won the greatest lottery of all! Face it, Tiger, I just hit the jackpot!

Before that momentous day in 1972, I was just another comics fan haunting his local newsstands awaiting the new releases. To be invited to the place where dreams were made was almost beyond anything I could've ever imagined happening to me. While Manhattan was just a ride away on the #6 subway line, it was also another world to this kid who grew up in the Bronx River Housing Projects. One of my dreams back then was to someday work for Marvel Comics. Little did I suspect that it would come true so soon.

I arrived at the appointed time, and I'm sure I was as nervous as can be. Or as they used to say back then, I was freaking out—but in a really good way and trying my best not to show it. To put it plainly, I was about to meet my gods. I was taken on a tour of the Marvel Bullpen by none other than Jazzy Johnny Romita himself, one of the greatest AMAZING SPIDER-MAN artists ever, and he introduced me to everyone. Eventually I was brought to an office where my new job was explained to me. All the while I was painfully aware that in the office just a few feet away was Smiling Stan Lee—live and in person.

That day changed my life forever. For the following twenty years I was a pit bull who had locked my jaw's on Marvel's ankle and I wasn't about to let go. For the first half of those twenty years I had a front row seat to the Greatest Show on Earth—watching Stan Lee and the rest of the Marvel Bullpen take that tiny company and build it into what it eventually became today. A giant force in the world of entertainment—and a major part of Disney.

To best illustrate my relationship with Stan, I like to recall how many years later, he dubbed me "The Wart," explaining that I was like a wart on his back side—every time he turned around there I was. But, I preferred to interpret that nickname as high praise. After all, didn't Merlin, the wise and powerful wizard in T. H. White's "The Once and Future King" call young King Arthur... the Wart?

And now here we are, working together again, this time at Papercutz, on a new generation of heroes—Steven Lee and his Zodiac team. Further proof that dreams really do come true!

'Nuff said!

STAY IN TOUCH!

EMAIL: salicrup@papercutz.com
WEB: papercutz.com
TWITTER: @papercutzgn
INSTAGRAM: @papercutzgn
FACEBOOK: PAPERCUTZGRAPHICNOVELS
FANMAIL: Papercutz, 160 Broadway,
         Suite 700, East Wing,
         New York, NY 10038

STAN LEE
Creator

As if co-creating the Marvel Universe with such characters as Spider-Man, The Avengers, The X-Men, Daredevil, The Incredible Hulk, Dr. Strange, and countless others, wasn't enough, Stan created a new generation of heroes with THE ZODIAC LEGACY!

STUART MOORE
Writer

Co-Author of THE ZODIAC LEGACY prose novels, Stuart is a writer and an award-winning comics editor.

P.H. MARCONDES
Artist

P.H. has been with Papercutz almost since the beginning illustrating such best-selling titles as THE HARDY BOYS, LEGO® NINJAGO, and SABAN'S THE POWER RANGERS.

ANDIE TONG
Cover Artist

Illustrator of THE ZODIAC LEGACY prose novel, he's a comic artist, multi-media designer, and book illustrator.